Praise for *This Tim...*

"Swoonily romantic and heartbreak...
—Katie Cotugno, *New York Times* b...

"I need this book right now. I'll read anything Lauren Gibaldi
writes."—Eric Smith, author of *Inked*, literary agent, and writer/
contributor for Paste magazine and BookRiot

"A worthy recommendation for fans of Sarah Dessen's
The Moon and More."—ALA *Booklist*

"Engaging and enjoyable."—*SLJ*

Praise for *Autofocus*

"*Autofocus* hit all the right notes, leaving me satisfied and
smiling."—Trish Doller, author of *Where the Stars Still Shine*

"A beautifully told story about friendship, family, and finding yourself. I couldn't stop turning pages."—Lauren Morrill, author of
The Trouble with Destiny

"A beautifully written story that takes you on an emotional ride."
—Eric Smith, author of *Inked*, literary agent, and writer/
contributor for Paste magazine and BookRiot

"Gibaldi gives voice to the fears and expectations of many
teenagers. Perfect for fans of Stephanie Perkins and Sarah Dessen
who are looking for a new author to love."—*SLJ*

"Has depth and pathos."—*Kirkus Reviews*

Praise for *The Night We Said Yes*

"Gibaldi effectively captures intense, all-consuming teen attraction."—*SLJ*

"Gibaldi's special debut will make readers ruminate on first chances, first loves, and those big, life-altering decisions. This perfectly paced book is fun to read, and the love story embedded within—along with a boatload of awesome characters—will appeal to lovers of all genres."—RT Book Reviews

"A story of friendship and romance, music and trespassing, and ultimately pursuing your own dream and your heart's desire. This romantic adventure has appeal, especially for fans of books like *Nick & Norah's Infinite Playlist*."—ALA *Booklist*

"The book speaks to the power of friendship and the importance of nurturing relationships."—*VOYA*

"A light but meaningful summer romance."—*Kirkus Reviews*

"Lauren Gibaldi so cleverly weaves the past and the present to tell an authentic, spontaneous story of friendship, romance, and all the gray areas in between. With the turn of each page, you'll be so glad you said yes to *The Night We Said Yes*!"—Julie Murphy, *New York Times* bestselling author of *Side Effects May Vary* and *Dumplin'*

Also by Lauren Gibaldi
The Night We Said Yes
Autofocus
Matt's Story (e-novella)

THIS
TINY
PERFECT
WORLD

LAUREN GIBALDI

HARPER TEEN
An Imprint of HarperCollins Publishers

To Colure Caulfield, Michelle Carroll, and Megan Donnelly:
for making my tiny world absolutely perfect.

"That time is short and it doesn't return again.
It is slipping away while I write this and while you read it,
and the monosyllable of the clock is Loss, loss, loss, unless
you devote your heart to its opposition."
—"The Catastrophe of Success," Tennessee Williams

ONE

I rest my head on Logan's shoulder as we watch the first summer sunset. The Florida air is thick, hot like the sidewalk we're sitting on, but that doesn't keep us from staying outside. After all of junior year in our suffocating, too brightly lit school, we need some time to breathe.

A familiar jingle echoes through the street, and from beside us Faye yells, "ICE CREAM!" In a flash she's up, running to the end of the block with all eight kids who were playing street ball following her. I laugh as she pretends to get exhausted so they beat her. And I smile as I see her pay for one of them. Big treats don't come often in our neighborhood, so Faye likes to dole out small surprises every now and then to the kids she babysits for.

Logan's arm wraps around my waist and the other hand

throws a baseball in the air, catching it in tune to the ice-cream truck's jingle. "Can all of summer be like this?" he asks.

"I wish," I say, thinking back to the last two summers, and how the three of us spent almost every day at the Springs, running along the trails, gripping the coarse rope swing over the water, swimming down low through the muck to see if we could find the underground caves, and jumping every time we saw something that resembled an alligator.

We sit in silence. It's one thing that's changed since we started dating two years ago—before we were always on, always talking or laughing or going on about something. Now we're just happy being . . . us. At first I worried we'd used up all our words, but I came to realize it's natural. And, mostly, it's comfortable, a kind of comfortable I'd never felt before.

After a few minutes, Faye returns with a kid on her back. His shaggy brown hair covers his wide eyes, and his thin arms wrap around Faye's neck.

"Make way for my captive!" Faye announces in a pirate voice, her red bandanna headband tied to make her look the part. "This here be Joshie, and Joshie must walk the plank."

"NO!" he laughs.

I play along, detangling myself from Logan and asking, "What be his crime?"

"Too much sugar," she says, dropping him.

"Nuh-uh! I only had one candy stick. One time I had

TWO candy sticks and I was like *ahhhh* and one was green, and the other was green."

"TWO greens?" Logan asks.

"YEAH!" Joshie shouts. "OH, can I play with the baseball?"

"Only if you can catch it," Logan taunts, hopping up and taking off around the dusty cul-de-sac as Joshie chases him.

After a beat, Faye sits down next to me, dropping her smile and fixing her hair back into a high knot. "It's gross how much you love all this right now." And there she is, the real Faye. She may be all sunshine and rainbows to the kids she babysits, but to me she's doom and gloom. And I love that about her—how she can somehow balance the two evenly.

"Summer? No school? Yes, I'm in love," I say dramatically, with my arms spread out.

"Not summer, nerd. This," she says, gesturing toward Logan. "Him all cute playing with Joshie."

"Shut up." I nudge her, then lean back on my hands, feeling the gravel dig into my skin. "I mean, it's not a bad thing." Because it *is* cute how he can jump and run and be one of the kids. He's always been that way in all of the ten years I've known him, happy around everyone and just incredibly fun. "But it's *this* I love. Us. All being here and hanging out. You know that's my favorite."

"Uh-huh."

"I'm serious!"

"But it's made even better because Logan is here," she says, batting her eyes and stretching out his name as long as possible.

I go along with her, because she's not completely incorrect. "He is pretty great, isn't he?"

"He's Logan," she says, stretching her tanned legs in front of her.

"And we're pretty great together, right?"

"Yes, you are the picture of perfection," she deadpans.

"And, once again, it's all thanks to you," I point out with a fake swoon.

"And once again, all I did was tell you guys on a daily basis that you're in love and should get married already—"

"Which wasn't weird or awkward or anything."

". . . until he finally got the balls to make a move."

"Please leave my boyfriend and his—"

"Balls?"

"Yes. Alone. Shut up." I smirk, suppressing a laugh.

"I love your swearing avoidance. I'm so using that to my advantage from now on."

"Remind me again why we're friends?"

"Because you looooove me," she says. I tap my foot to hers, and think back to when she and I met in science class in ninth grade. She kept making fun of me for not wanting to dissect a frog until I finally told her to shut up. And it was like a dam broke and she had just been waiting for me to stand up for myself. We've been inseparable ever since.

"So, this is a cool job," I say, changing the subject. "You just watch the kids for a few hours and get paid?" I look out at the kids running about the cul-de-sac, around the houses, ducking around old tires and wooden fences.

"Pretty much, yeah. Since I already babysit most of them, the parents asked if I could watch them all at once every now and then, so they could eat in peace or whatever. So I watch them play outside until it's time to go in. It's an easy gig. I mean, I'm just hanging out. Plus it gets me out of my house and away from my dad, so, you know . . ."

"And you can have company," I quickly add, not wanting her to dwell on her family issues.

"And I can have company," she agrees, smiling and wiping her hands on her shorts. She looks up at the kids a few steps away playing four corners (despite there being no corners) and has such a look of pride. She's seen them all practically grow up; she's invested.

Logan runs over and as I wave, he tackles me at the waist, forcing me backward onto the grass. I let out a quick yell that turns into a laugh.

"Gotcha," he says, kissing me lightly on the lips, before pulling me back up. An "ooohhh" comes out from some of the kids, and I blush but still hold on to him.

"Children, children," Faye says, not even glancing in our direction.

5

"Sorry, Mom," Logan says, resuming his place next to me on the curb. "So, Joshie can really run. I'm totally out of breath."

"Maybe he should take your spot on the baseball team next year?" I joke.

"I should start training him now," he muses.

"Not everyone wants to be a jock," Faye retorts.

"Yeah, maybe he'll be an actor," I challenge.

"Or in a band," Faye continues.

"Maybe Joshie will hate sports."

"But not green candy sticks."

"No, he'll never hate green candy sticks," I laugh.

"I give up with you two." He shakes his head. He's wearing his baseball team's hat, and his red hair peeks out from under it.

"Loooove youuuuu," I say, as cheesy as possible, and he rests his chin on my head.

A kid waves for us to watch, and we all focus our attention on two girls doing cartwheels at the same time. We cheer and applaud and make them feel like they're as special as can be.

"So, Logan, what're you up to this summer?" Faye asks.

"Working," he says, leaning back. "Brad got me a job at the bounce-house rental place he works for."

"I want to say something cynical, but that's actually pretty cool. I love bounce houses."

"Right? As far as summer jobs go, it's pretty ace," he says.

"But Penny's jealous of all the birthday parties I'm going to go to."

I roll my eyes and with an exaggerated sigh add, "He may leave me for a five-year-old."

"How much is it to rent one of them, anyway?" Faye asks.

"Like a hundred plus dollars. It's insane. Who can spend that much on a party?" he answers.

"I have no idea," Faye says, shaking her head and facing our neighborhood, with its yellowing grass and tiny cookie-cutter houses. I used to want all the cool toys some of my other friends had, but somehow realized that my mom's job at the restaurant and Dad's at the school couldn't make them afford everything. So I stopped hoping for the fancy dresses and tickets to touring Broadway shows. I didn't let it bother me. But something about high school makes you want a little more. Which is why I started working at the restaurant, and Faye began babysitting, and Logan got this summer job. But this summer is going to be different. I still feel guilty leaving the restaurant, but the acting camp I'm going to is a once-in-a-lifetime opportunity. Not many people get accepted, and when I did, I couldn't say no. "So Logan's working, I'm babysitting, and you're acting," Faye says, waving at the parents as they start calling their kids in.

"Correct," I say, waving, too.

"It's the first summer we're not all just—"

"Hanging out," I finish for her.

She pauses, then says, "Yeah."

It is weird, knowing that tomorrow we'll all be off doing something else. We won't be together every moment of the day. Logan rubs my hand silently, and I think we're all picturing the same thing. The summer spread out ahead of us, with all its possibilities. For us together . . . and apart.

And that's how it should be, I guess. Moving forward, apart but still together. We may do different things, but I know we'll always go back to one another.

After all, we have it all planned out—our futures here.

Together.

◇◇◇◇

We say our good-byes and Logan walks me the mile from Faye's house back to mine. Sometimes, in the dead of summer, when it feels like I'm cooking from the heat rising off the ground and the mosquitos are swirling around my head, I wish the walk were quicker, and that we lived closer to one another. But tonight, I wish for more time so we can make the most of our last night before summer really starts.

"What're you thinking?" I ask him, just to make conversation. Our hands, linked between us, swing.

"Remember in our last game, when Brad hit that foul ball so far back it hit the people behind home plate?"

"Yeah?" I ask, wondering where this is going.

"He denied doing it—said he never hit a foul. Played a perfect season."

"When'd he say that?"

"Yesterday, when I met up with him to get my schedule."

"Why'd he lie to you about it?"

He grinned and rolled his eyes. "A girl was at the shop. So you know him."

"Mm-hmmm," I nod, feeling a bit of apprehension in my stomach. Brad is the worst kind of guy, always hitting on girls, always bragging about his "conquests," as he calls them. Seriously, the worst. "So glad you're spending *all* summer with him."

"Ah, he's fine. I'm just gonna have to get used to, like, covering for him or whatever."

"Didn't he cheat on his last, like, three girlfriends?"

"I didn't say he was perfect. But he's a solid teammate and a good friend." When I don't answer, he stops walking and asks, "Wait, you know I won't— I'm not like him."

"No, no, I know that." I shake my head. I know Logan isn't like that. He was dumped by his last girlfriend, during our freshman year, after she hinted about them breaking up for months. I tried talking to him about it, but he was in denial. He's loyal to a fault, I guess. I tug on his hand and start walking again, turning onto my long, dark, quiet street. Cicadas buzz in the night sky. "Sooooo, are you excited about work?"

"Yeah, kind of. I mean, it's fine. It's just a job."

"I'm sure your mom appreciates you working and helping her out."

"Yeah, totally. She's received zero child support for me

and Mikey in the last million years or whatever, so I want to help."

"That really sucks . . ." I start, but I know not to go further.

"Anyway," he says, changing the subject. "What about you? All set for tomorrow?"

"I guess," I say with a shrug. "I'm really excited, but also . . ."

"Don't say nervous. You're never nervous."

"I'm not *not* nervous. How's that?"

"You're gonna kill it," he says, and I hope he's right. But I *am* scared. I auditioned for Breakthrough Theatre Camp on a whim—several of my theater friends were trying out, so I thought I would, too. I didn't think I'd actually get in. But I just felt like I had to audition—I can never get the feeling of being onstage out of my mind. The jitters beforehand, the calm onstage, the chance to be someone else. And somehow . . . I got into the camp. I cried when I found out.

Growing up, everyone had *something*. Even now, Logan has his baseball. Faye loves taking care of kids. All my other friends had singing, or instruments, or dance. And I didn't have anything. And then, when I got into high school, acting just clicked—like it was something I could do, something I was good at.

"Thank you," I finally say and give his hand a squeeze. "I hope everyone is cool there."

"They're gonna be quoting Shakespeare and, like, *The Book of Mormon* in the hallways. You're gonna fit right in."

"Awww, you remembered the name of a musical."

"I listen sometimes." He grins. We've had a long-standing agreement that we won't talk too much about baseball or theater. But of course we break it all the time. He can name Jean Valjean's inmate number in *Les Misérables*, one of my favorite shows. I know the typical starting lineup for the Florida Marlins.

"I *am* really excited," I say, thinking about tomorrow, and feeling a bubbling of emotion. "I think it'll be amazing. But . . . I still kind of feel bad about leaving the diner."

"Your dad said it was fine; what's there to worry about?"

I shake my head. "I don't know. Him?"

"He'll be fine. The diner will be fine. *You'll* be fine."

"I know, I know. I don't know why I'm so worried. I guess . . . day-before nerves or whatever." I pause. "And I'm still thinking about what Faye said."

He scratches his head, moving his hat all around. "About us being apart this summer?"

"Yeah. Cheesy, I know, but we've had so much fun every summer since . . ."

"Since the summer you threw a baseball at my head when we were, what, seven?"

"I didn't throw it at your head. I threw it to your hand, and your head got in the way."

"You threw it at my head because you thought I was the hottest guy in the park and you wanted an excuse to talk to me."

"You were in third grade. You were far from hot," I say, poking him in the side, and he slides his arm around my shoulders and stops walking again.

"You were totally into my big glasses."

"My weakness." I fake swoon.

He pulls me close, and I look up and see him at all our stages throughout our years together. Our skinned-knees-just-friends-middle-school phase when I'd hang out at his house after school, waiting for my mom to pick me up. Or, later, after she died, my dad. Our new-to-high-school-and-scared phase where we'd parade through the woods and recount our day after the school bus dropped us off. Our pretending-to-not-like-each-other phase that drove us apart until longing brought us back together. And I wonder if it all was meant to lead to here.

He leans down and kisses me under the buzzing streetlamp, and I think, yeah, maybe it was.

◇◇◇◇

By the time I get home, the house is mostly quiet, except for the TV in my dad's bedroom. I go to knock once and tell him I'm home, but I realize it's not the TV—it's his voice. He must be on the phone.

"Soon, I promise, soon."

Curiosity gets the best of me, so I creep closer to his door.

"I'll think it over. I just . . . I don't know about right now."

I lean forward and forget about the one creaky spot. The noise rings out, and I hurry to my room, not waiting for him to think I was spying. Even though I kind of was.

"Pen?"

I jump on my bed, throw my shoes into my closet, and grab the closest book to me.

"Pen?" I hear again.

"In here," I call back, trying to keep my voice normal.

I hear him before I see him—his slippers flip-flopping on the hardwood floors. He pokes his head in my room and looks like he's had a day. His graying black hair is sticking up in the back from him pulling at it, I'm sure, and his face needs a shave. "Hey. Didn't hear you come in."

"Sorry," I say, realizing I should have run to the front door and announced my return, instead of sneaking into my room. "Got in a few minutes ago and wanted to take my shoes off. Blisters from the heat."

"Oh," he says, looking relieved. As if he's worried I'd overheard something. Like I did. I want to ask him about it, but he looks so tired. "Have fun with Faye?"

"And Logan, yeah. We just hung out while Faye baby-sat." He makes a "humph" noise. "Dad, it's been almost two years—you have to be used to me having a boyfriend by now."

"I don't have to be used to anything," he says.

"It's not like Logan is suddenly around or anything. You

13

do remember that Mom used to let him sleep over in my room when we were little."

I say it so easily, it just slips out really, and both of us feel it, a chill going up our spines. We've gotten to the point that we can talk about Mom openly. Remember her fondly. But it's still hard, even today, five years after she died in the car accident. There's still a gaping absence.

Still, he smiles at the memory, leaning against my door with his arms crossed. "I never agreed with that, of course. Y'all were so quiet in here, I used to stand by the door and listen in."

"You were *spying* on us? You know we were just playing board games, right?"

"Doesn't mean a dad can't worry." He drops his arms, as if the weight of worrying was physically too much. "Excited about tomorrow?"

I shake my head at his discomfort and the subject change. "Yeah, definitely."

"Great, well, rest up. I'll have breakfast ready for you before you go, okay?"

"Won't you be at work?"

"A dad can see his daughter off on her first day, right?" I smile, knowing it's something my mom would have done and said, too. She was always at the restaurant—her restaurant—but she made time for me, for us. For special occasions. She always took off for them. Before she died, Dad worked at the high school as a guidance counselor. But after, he felt like he owed it to Mom to take over the Country Time Café. And to me, to keep it going until I was ready to have it. He had barely any restaurant experience, but has been able to keep the place running, employed, and populated.

"Okay, sleep well, honey."

"Thanks, Dad. You too."

When I hear the click of the door, I get up and go to my closet.

In the back corner I find the small, spiral-bound notepad. It was a weird thing to keep, but I never saw Mom without it. And it has her writing in it. When you lose someone, you never see their writing again, their notes. So even though it just has lists of things she needed to do or buy for the café, I love looking at it, seeing the importance of milk (underlined three times) and the repetition of flour. I love feeling the pages, the indentation from her pressing too hard with her black pen. I flip to the beginning page and see it there—in her writing, "Make Today Count."

I keep that in mind when I put the book away, change into pajamas, and climb into bed. Yes, I feel guilty not helping out at the restaurant this summer, but I feel Mom would approve of what I'm doing. I know she'd cheer me on, just like Dad. I'm doing what feels right. I'm making my summer count.

TWO

Just as promised, Dad is in the kitchen the next morning, standing in front of the microwave with the newspaper and a mug of coffee in his hand, and a stack of pancakes waiting for me.

"There's no way I'm eating all of that," I say, sitting at the small kitchen table and picking up the syrup.

"Who says they're all for you?"

"Are there guests I don't know about?" I joke, and for a second wonder what that would be like—Dad bringing someone home, having her stay the night. Thank god he hasn't done that yet.

"If there were, they'd be very grateful for my pancakes." He joins me at the table and points to the newspaper. "Looks like a new breakfast place is opening this weekend. Some fancy chain."

"How close?"

"One block from our café."

"Oh," I say, shaking my head at the thought of competition. Our place does fine—not extraordinary, but not terrible. There are longtime regulars that keep it populated, and every now and then a new person. "Are you worried?"

"Competition is competition. But does that place have famous chickens hanging around behind the building? I don't think so."

I laugh, picturing the "I Break for Christmas Chickens" bumper stickers Mom had made. No one knows where the chickens come from, or where they go. But everyone feeds them.

"How're Tony and the crew holding up without you today?"

He shrugs and sits at the table with me. "Surviving. I'll head over there in a little bit. Do you want me to drive you to camp today?"

"No, no," I say, pancake in my mouth. "It's like a forty-five-minute drive. I'll take the bus."

"You sure? You don't know anyone else going, right? Anyone from school that you could carpool with?"

"Nope, it's just me. Which is surprising because there are so many better actors at school. Like, how was my audition so much better than theirs?"

"You're excellent," he says, leaning back on the chair and crossing his arms.

"And you're my dad, so you have to say that."

"I'm your dad, and I *choose* to say it."

"Well, fine, but remember *Brighton Beach Memoirs*? The leads in that were amazing, and they didn't get in. And, like, no one from our production of *Grease*."

"Maybe they saw something in you that they didn't see with the others. Also, the leads in *Grease* were only okay. Danny's dancing was atrocious."

I cover my mouth from laughing. "It was not!"

"And Rizzo stopped singing during her song!"

"Yeah, but . . . Okay, you're right. The night you came really sucked. The others were better!"

"I'll just take your word for it." He chuckles.

I look up at the time. "Crap, running late." I shovel in a few more bites, then run back to my room. As I finish getting ready, I think back to my audition.

There were about ten of us from school that applied and auditioned, and only I made it. Maybe there is a reason. Or maybe it's pure luck. But it was the most intimidating moment of my life, standing in front of real directors who worked with real stars. I passed with my monologue from *A Doll's House* where my character leaves her husband, wondering if he ever truly loved her, or just this image of her. It was powerful and hard and made me cry, and I think that was what did it. I'd performed it in my acting class at school, after working on it for months. My school director said crying was the key, but only if I meant it.

The day of the audition, I meant it. It was the anniversary of my mom's death, and though it'd been five years, it still felt raw, like it'd happened yesterday.

So I got in, also receiving the scholarship I applied for, and promptly freaked out to Logan. He demanded we celebrate with pizza, so we went to the place with the real plates instead of paper.

I take what feels like seven hundred hours getting ready, picking out the right outfit that says *I'm serious*, but also *I can play any age, really, just give me a shot*. I settle on a black dress with a white Peter Pan collar that Faye helped me pick out at a thrift store for photo day last year. I pair it with a red bow headband holding my black hair back. With my bangs, maybe I look French. Mysterious. New.

Like I could be someone else.

I grab my bag off my dresser along with my keys and head out, passing Dad's door on the way.

"Leaving!"

"Love you!" he yells, then pops his head out, phone in his hand. "Have a good day."

"You too." I nod to the phone. "Told you they couldn't survive without you." His brows go down, lips pucker, a look of confusion. "Country Time?"

"Oh! Yeah." He nods. "They didn't know where I put the extra salt."

"You'd think they would." I shake my head, then head out the door. I walk to the end of my block and turn right onto the main street toward the bus stop. Holiday signs decorate the lampposts, even though it's June. Despite being called "Christmas," the city is far from festive, especially this time of the year, when it's hotter than the sun. Still, it's home. A gray-haired shirtless man with bug-like eyes whistles as I walk by, but I hold my head higher, hoping he doesn't see my eye roll, or the pink spreading across my face.

There are a few people at the bus stop, regulars from the neighborhood on their way to work or the library, where there's free AC. I wave, then rummage through my bag, looking for my bus pass and headphones.

In a puff of exhaust, the bus pulls up and I sit near the front, looking out the window, soundtrack to *In the Heights* playing on my earbuds. I've been taking the bus on and off since middle school, but today feels different. Like something is about to happen. Something noteworthy.

I'm leaving behind the small houses and dingy crabgrass-filled yards and going to Winter Park, the fanciest neighborhood in central Florida. There are mansions and former celebrities and a Park Avenue. Their lakes have boat tours and waterskiing; our lakes have gators and algae. It's there that Breakthrough Theatre Camp is located, within a small liberal arts college. It's known for raising "real actors," ones that can go to Broadway or Los Angeles feeling confident.

I get off the bus right outside the college and start walking toward the theater when my phone vibrates.

You didn't.

I smile, knowing Logan got my surprise. It's a link to a playlist of all our favorite songs, with a note for each song. My "Perfect Morning" mix for him. I'd prepared it a few days ago, and emailed it to him first thing this morning.

I did. ☺

You're the best. I'm listening to it right now.

Sing along for me.

Break a leg. You're gonna rock it.

I smile again, knowing there will be a piece of me with him today as he has his first day of work. I breathe in deep and walk under a brick archway, and onto the tree-lined campus.

The college is small, but to me it feels huge. I'm surrounded by green fields and coral-and-tan-shaded buildings. There's a soccer field to my left, a parking lot to my right, and sidewalks snaking all around. Students are walking through campus, I guess going to summer school. There's a building that actually has a gargoyle peering over it. I pull out my phone and type the name of the auditorium into the map app. It says it's to the left, so I walk in that direction until I find myself standing in front of a giant red-roofed building with a big sign announcing the camp's dates. Fear and excitement race through my body as my face bursts into a grin. Up a flight of stairs are three archways in a row, leading to the entrance of the theater. I take a deep breath and walk up the stairs, passing a few people my age who stop talking to watch me.

I shake my fears away—fears of being new, of not being good enough, of not fitting in—straighten my dress, and brace myself before going inside.

The lobby is tan like the outside. There's a ticket counter with a few tables and chairs set up. Posters from previous performances cover the walls. *Little Shop of Horrors, Gypsy, Hamlet*. A few eyes catch mine, and I notice a guy with spiky blond hair giving me a once-over before he follows everyone else through a door into the auditorium. So I follow, too.

Voices are magnified once I'm inside. There aren't many of us, maybe thirty in all, sitting in the first few rows. I take a seat in the second row on the aisle and look around nervously, seeing if, at least maybe, there's a familiar face from somewhere. An acting competition. A play I saw at another school. No luck. But while I pass by faces, I remember that I'm in a real theater. A real playhouse. And a startling realization hits me—everyone here might go on to do something big. I could be looking at future Broadway or movie stars.

A woman, who I remember from my audition, comes out onstage, and I hear some cheers and hoots, so I guess there are a lot of people here who are returning. She gestures for them to quiet down as she sits on the stage, legs hanging off.

"Welcome to Breakthrough," she says with a deep voice and giant smile. She's wearing all black, so her deep maroon hair stands out. "I'm so excited to have all of you here this summer. Auditions were very hard this year, there was some stiff competition, but I know we picked the best. I'm Teresa Walker, for those who don't know me, and I'll be one of your acting coaches, as well as the director of one of the shows. As you know, we will perform two shows in eight weeks. I'll be working on the dramatic play, which is Tennessee Williams's *The Glass Menagerie*."

Excited whispers fill the room. I've heard of the play, but haven't read it. Worry creeps up over me. Maybe I should've done some pre-camp reading.

"The other show is *Spring Awakening*." More, louder cheers. "Auditions will be in two weeks. Everyone will have a part in one of the shows, be it the main cast or as an understudy, or part of the production team. And it goes without saying, but not everyone will have a lead. So work hard. Impress us."

The room is silent, and I'm nodding along, taking in

every word she says. She goes on to describe the camp, how we'll have acting, vocal, and movement/dance classes each day, along with rehearsals for whichever show we're cast in. Even as understudies we're guaranteed one night of performance. We'll have guest speakers and trainers throughout the summer, coming from New York and L.A., former students and former teachers of our teachers. It's so different from what my summer could have been. It feels like I'm in a warped version of reality.

By the time her welcome speech is over, I'm ready to fly, practically. With everyone else, I make my way up the aisle and out the doors back into the lobby.

"Okay, crew," a man in the front yells. I recognize him as someone also at my audition. He's older, about my dad's age, with a graying beard and a pierced ear. "Classes will be in the building next door. Last names A–M go to the first room on your right, N–Z first room on your left."

With my N last name, I follow him back outside to the bright sun, and inside a brick building with doors lining both sides. With half the students, I filter into the left-side room and am greeted with a big, open bright white room. Chairs, couches, and beanbags are all spaced out, which makes it more comfortable than stark. It smells like paint, like the room was just transformed into this.

I head to a chair and sit, putting my bag down and taking out my notebook, ready to soak everything up.

The same man walks up and kind of paces around, taking

in all of our faces. "I'm Miles Stone," he says. "Call me Miles. All of us teachers will be rotating this summer, but you have the first couple of weeks of acting with me. I recognize quite a few faces. Raise your hand if you're returning."

I quickly look around and see about five hands go up, roughly one-third of the people in the room, which is pretty intimidating.

Miles nods, rubbing his hand over his beard and pacing around. "Great. Then you know what I expect out of my classes. Everyone else, this'll be a ride." I shift in my seat, part nervous, part ready to get started.

"The thing about acting is that you always have to be ready. You never know if something will go wrong in a show; you just have to jump in and make it work. The point of this class is to get you prepared. Real actors are always prepared." He stops pacing right in front of me, then calls out, "You two."

I look around to see if anyone else moves, but everyone is looking at me and the girl to my left. Oh. Good.

The girl gets up with a bounce and looks excitedly at me. I take a deep breath, then stand up and follow her. When we get to the front of the classroom, she bounces in place and gives me a panicked but happy grin, and for some reason, that calms me.

"Great. Names?"

"Sam."

"Penny," I say.

"Sam and Penny, I remember you both from auditions. I chose you because I liked your styles. Daring, spontaneous." He turns back to the class and I wonder which one of us is daring, and which one is spontaneous. "This is your acting class. In here is a safe space. We're going to make changes. We're going to push boundaries. And we're going to get results. *You're* going to get results. Are you two ready?"

"Um," I say nervously, as Sam answers, "Yes."

"Great. Read this," Miles says, giving us each a sheet of paper. It's a short script, only four lines each. I read it over quickly, and look up at Sam.

Role one? she mouths, pointing to herself. I nod and take role two.

"And . . . action," Miles says.

"I don't know how to tell you this, but . . ." Sam starts, and I realize she's reading from the script. I can't believe I'm about to act in front of people after only a few seconds of looking at a script. I've been in three shows, competed in one competition, and even done a bit of improvisation work, but nothing has been this intense. A flush rises over my cheeks. I look at her, and though she sounds confident, I can see that her eyes are wide, her hands shaking. I look down to notice mine moving, too.

Sam finishes and gives me a look that encourages me to continue. So I hold on tightly to my script and read, "You did what?"

My voice comes out shaky and hoarse, like I haven't

spoken in years. My face flushes again and Sam continues. I look down and reread my next line, trying to say it a few times in my head before she reaches the end of hers.

There's a long pause, and I realize she's waiting for me, so I start reading the line, and trip over my words a few times. I clear my voice and continue, but my nerves won't go away. I can't concentrate on what the words mean because I'm so focused on just getting them out.

Sam does her remaining lines, and I do mine, and by the time we're finished I'm sweating like I just ran a race. I've never been so tense in my life. I'm pretty sure I failed whatever test this was, and I close my eyes, waiting for Miles to say I'm kicked out due to such an embarrassing performance.

"Class, what do you think?" Miles asks before giving any sort of assessment.

I open my eyes and look at the faces staring at us, but no one says a word; no one moves. Finally, one hand goes up, and I see that it's the blond spiky-haired guy from the lobby.

"Yes, go ahead," Miles says.

"Okay, well, it was fine, but they weren't acting, right? They were just reading the lines. There was no emotion or anything."

I cringe from his words. It's exactly what I was thinking.

"You're exactly right," Miles says, and my heart plummets. I drop my head in despair, not wanting anyone to see my red cheeks. "But that's no fault to the actors. I gave them no warning, no preparation. They did fine with what they had. Being able to act—*truly act*—with no warning is something you have to work at, develop. And that's what we're going to do here. We're going to develop you, not just as actors while you're in the moment, but also when you're not. By the end of this camp, you'll feel new and always on."

He turns to us. "You two may sit down."

I walk back to my seat, relieved. Sam gives me an encouraging glance, and I half smile back. I have no idea how she's so perky after that performance. Well, she was at least pretty good. As I pass the blond guy, he gives me a nod, and my smile vanishes.

Miles starts telling us a story about a former student, and though I'm paying attention, I'm also readying myself. For the summer. For learning everything I can. I look back at the blond guy, who's now leaning back comfortably on his beanbag chair and grinning, and know none of this will be easy.

THREE

We stick with the same people for each of our classes, so when I get into vocal class, I walk over and sit next to Sam.

She quickly turns to me and says, "So, that was crazy embarrassing."

"Seriously." I shake my head. "But you were really good."

"What? No. I've been put on the spot before, but that was, like, *intense.*"

"I was convinced I was about to be kicked out," I admit with a smile.

"I was convinced I was going to be burned at the stake."

"Glad we were in it together, then," I say.

"We can be partners in failure, or something." She chuckles, like the anxiety from earlier is all gone.

"Excellent!" I say, then "I'm Penny."

"Sam! It's my first year. Yours?"

"Yeah, which I think is a little too obvious."

"Nah." She waves me off. "I think everyone's nervous . . . even if they don't show it."

The blond guy walks in and I quietly say, "That was super nice how he called us out."

She shrugs. "Just finding a way to stand out." Then, in a whisper, she adds, "He's, like, really hot, though."

I laugh because, hey, consolation prize.

At the front of the room, Teresa, our instructor, starts shuffling some sheet music. When most of the seats are filled, and no one else is coming in, she closes her eyes and starts playing the piano. I instantly know the song: "Seasons of Love" from the musical *RENT*. I feel the words in my mouth, and suppress my desire to sing along. I've embarrassed myself once today—I'm not doing it again. Next to me, Sam is moving in her seat, also feeling the music, and beyond her, a few others are doing the same, some mouths also sounding out the words.

"Measure in looooooooove." One voice starts singing the chorus, and I turn around to see that it's a girl with big hair and a bigger voice standing on a chair. With that, it's like a dam explodes and everyone joins in, lending their voices to the mix. A bellowing soprano comes next to me and I see it's Sam, whose eyes are closed and who's as confident as can be. I let the feeling come over me until I, too, am singing. My voice isn't great, but I know being here and playing safe won't cut it. So I sing louder, braver.

The song ends and we all cheer, applauding each other. The girl on the chair takes a bow, and Teresa turns around and smiles at us.

"Now, that wasn't so hard, was it?" she asks, and we all giggle. "That is what I want out of this class. Not just the ability to sing, but also the bravery to be the first person to sing. The ability to join in when asked, or when not asked. That passionate feeling in every song. I want all of that."

I nod my head with everything she says, knowing I'm going to have to work at this. I'm not classically trained—I've never had singing lessons like some of the people here have, and I've only been in my school chorus a couple of years—so I'm excited to get these tips and see how I'll improve by the end of summer.

After, we move on to the next class, movement, which is more of the same—an introduction to dances we'll learn and the push to get us on our feet.

At the end of class, we follow our teacher back to the lobby, where the other class is filing in, too. Cliques form almost naturally. The loners wait on the sidelines. It's like high school, only in a different place. I stand next to Sam, and she doesn't move, and I feel like I might have just made my first friend here.

"All right!" Teresa waves to get our attention. "You've almost survived your first day. At this time, you'd go off to rehearse whichever show you're working on, or have independent time with one of us. Since it's the first day, we'll just have a get-to-know-you session. Feel free to walk around the facilities and take it all in. Meet your fellow actors. Get comfortable with one another, because it's going to be a long summer." She says it with a smile, but I almost think it's a threat.

"Shall we?" Sam asks, and I follow her to a table and grab a bottle of water. Then we lean against the wall and she shakes her head. "This place is amazing."

I guess with my nerves I never really looked at her, but now I see she matches perfectly with how she looks. Big voice, big personality, big glasses, big curls.

"Yeah! I'm still surprised I got in."

"Right? I can't wait until we start working on the shows," she says, looking around the room, her curls bouncing up and down.

"Speaking of," I say, pointing to her *Into the Woods* T-shirt, "I love that show."

"ME TOO!" she yells. "My school put it on last year. I was a stepsister. Were you in it?"

"No," I say. "Just seen the movie. Like, the old movie— the theater performance."

"Yeah, totally. The new one doesn't live up."

"Not at all." I smile.

"Penny, is it?" a voice asks from my left. I look at Sam, then turn around. It's the blond guy, cocking an eyebrow and rubbing his hands together. The same guy who embarrassed us earlier.

"Yes," I say, putting my hand on my hip as I turn to look at him. He's giving me a curious look, almost daring, almost like he's amused by my name and pushing to see if I'm lying. I'm not.

"Chase," he says, decidedly, sticking out his hands. "Chase Matthews. New to the area, new to the school." I look back at Sam quickly, remembering what she said about him, and grin. He *is* pretty cute up close, if arrogant.

"We're new, too!" Sam interjects, her unadulterated enthusiasm showing, and for a second I feel embarrassed for her. Chase doesn't look like the kind of guy who goes for enthusiasm.

"It's our first year at the camp," I say.

"Have you tried out before?" he asks, leaning an arm on our table.

"No," I say, and I see Sam shake her head, too.

"I did a few TV shows up in Atlanta, nothing big, so I thought I'd try out theater."

"So you have experience?" Sam asks incredulously. "Like, professional experience? On a TV show? Ohmygosh, what were you in? How was it? Was it amazing?"

33

"Yeah, Atlanta's a hub for acting right now. I had a few speaking roles on CW shows, but, you know, nothing huge," he says.

"Why're you here, then?" I ask. It comes out meaner than I intended.

"My dad's new job." He rolls his eyes. "I thought there'd be more here, but it looks like your screen stuff isn't happening right now. But whatever. I've only got a year left until I graduate, then I'm hitting up L.A."

Sam pipes in, "I'm going to New York after school—try my hand at Broadway. I'm going to apply to NYU and live in Greenwich Village. I have it all planned." She says it with so much conviction that, even barely knowing her, I believe it.

"Good luck." Chase scoffs, and then looks at me. "And you?"

"Oh, I don't know yet," I say, frustrated by his last remark. "I'm kind of happy here. Don't really have any plans to leave."

He shrugs and for a second I see the two of us through his eyes. Me, all bangs and limbs. Sam, a bit larger with a theater shirt on. We're not movie-star beautiful, we're just two girls trying. And I suddenly feel protective of that. Why should we have to live up to his expectations?

"I'm gonna go check out the stage," I say right at him. "Sam, want to come?"

"Yes! I want to see their fly system. Apparently last

summer they did *Peter Pan* and legit made a girl fly into the audience."

I smile and lead the way away from Chase. I'm still not even sure why he was talking to us. He may just be here to fill up time, but he's not going to take ours away.

FOUR

At the end of the day, I hop on the bus and sit against the window, watching the streets pass by as we leave. This morning I was all nerves and uncertainty. But now, I want to experience it all. I want to have fun. I pull out my phone to text Faye.

Survived first day!

Yesss. Didn't sing yourself to death?

Ha. Ha.

JK, how was it?

Really good! I like it a lot. There's acting and singing and

dancing . . . and we're gonna be in a show. It's really going to be amazing.

This sounds like heaven for you.

Right? Full summer of acting. Dream come true.

Glad it's so awesome.

It is, I think. It's still exciting that I get to do this all summer, instead of working. Even though she's been doing it for years, I forget that it's kind of Faye's first day of her summer job, too. I know she's happy babysitting, I know it's what she wants to do, but . . . I wonder if she wants to do something big and different, too.

How was your day?

Cool! I was vomited on by Joshie, so your day won.

Gross. Did he eat 2 candy sticks again?

Haha, no. Just sick.

Don't get sick.

TOO LATE.

I smile at her messages and shake my head. For the rest of the drive, I look up *The Glass Menagerie* on my phone—never too early to start getting ready.

When the bus pulls up to my stop, I see Logan's grinning face. "I thought you were working!" I say as he brings me into his arms.

"Got off early, so thought I'd surprise you." He kisses my head, and then wraps his arm around my shoulder as we walk toward home.

"How was your first day?" I ask.

"Weird. Cool, but weird. It's a lot of work."

"Good or bad work?" I ask.

"Is work ever good?" he asks. "It was fine. Lots of setting up and taking down. Nothing too hard. I got to try out some of the houses. I felt like I was five. I totally get why kids want them at their parties."

We pass a side-of-the-road fruit stand and I wave at the guy manning it. He's here every day selling strawberries or melons or, sometimes, pumpkins if it's the season.

We take a left down the wooded path and I pull him in closer as we walk and listen to the familiar birds chirping in the trees around us. "What about you? How was it?" The smell of BBQ sauce, from the place right off the bus stop, hits us and I know I'm home.

"Good. Weird, but good," I say, using his words with a smile. "It was inspiring. It feels awesome, you know, being around so many other actors."

"Singing in the halls? Flash mob during lunch?"

"No"—I push on his stomach—"though honestly I wouldn't be surprised if that did happen."

We walk over debris from a recent storm and sit on the ground, leaning against an overturned tree that's been here as long as I can remember. We used to climb on it when we were in the third grade, feeling the rough bark against our bare feet. Then it became our place to hide and talk when we needed to get away. Like when Logan's dad left. Or when my mom died.

"I missed you today." He kisses me and pushes my hair behind my ears. I smile. This is exactly where I want to be, but my mind keeps flashing back to my day at camp. His face changes, and he asks, "What's going on?"

"Nothing." I shake my head.

"Not thinking about all the new dudes you met, right? Should I be worried?" He grins and I push his hair out of his face.

"SO worried," I joke. "They can rap along to *Hamilton*, and you have yet to master that."

"My biggest flaw," he says. "But can they do this?" He kisses me again, rubbing his hand over my side.

"No, they cannot."

"Tell me about them," he says.

So I tell him about the teachers and Sam. "One guy kind of annoyed me," I say, meaning Chase. "He's new to Florida, and, you know, already hates it."

"Yeah, you have to give it time before you can hate it."

"Exactly," I say. "He's convinced he'll go off to Hollywood," I say, not really knowing why I added that.

Logan looks at me seriously, then asks, "You're not going to leave me for L.A., are you?"

"No, of course not." I'm a girl from small-town Florida—we stay here. I've never really seen anyone leave. We go to school here, then we run family businesses passed down for generations or work at places we were hired at in high school. It sounds small-town, and it is, but I like it. I like that I know the guy who sells strawberries on the side of the road. That the same family has owned the BBQ place down the street since my mom was a kid, and sometimes they'll give you ice pops for free if you ask nicely. I like that I'll have a place handed down to me.

I have a life here, a future. I don't need to leave.

I look up at Logan and smile, and kiss him until he believes me. "I'm not going anywhere."

When I get home, I hear Dad before I see him, typing on his computer in the kitchen. "Hey," I call out as I join him.

"Hold on, hold on," he says, putting one finger up as he finishes whatever he's working on. Everyone always says I look like my dad, and I really see it right now. We both have the same near-black hair, tan features. My mom was completely light—light brown hair, light gray eyes. Light skin.

Just light. "Okay, hi. How was your first day?" He shuts his laptop and rests back in his chair.

"It was great."

"Great? That's it?" he asks, crossing his arms across his chest expectantly.

I sit down across from him. I've already rehashed this with Logan, so I just summarize the day.

"Sounds like you've got quite the summer ahead of you."

"I seriously do. How was work?"

He sighs. "Fine—you know, the usual. The freezer needs to be replaced soon, which is . . ."

"Not cheap."

"No, right. So we'll see when something has to be done about that."

"Do you want me to help out this weekend?"

"We should have enough staff, but we'll see. You know how it is over the summer."

"Yeah," I say, remembering last summer, when I had to work pretty much every day for a few hours just as backup because the waiters were so swamped. I constantly came home smelling like bacon. "Well, let me know. I'm probably not doing anything."

I get up and head to my room, ready to just relax after the day. Across the room is my poster wall, where I hang all the flyers from shows I've been in, and the covers of programs from ones I've seen. It's cluttered, but I like it.

I check my email on my phone, and get a text from Faye.

Dad lost his job. Again.

Come over.

Before she even responds, I pop back outside and yell to my dad. "Hey, Faye's spending the night."

"On a school night?" he jokes.

"Her dad lost his job." There's silence because he knows what that means. Her dad will get drunk. Her dad will be angry. He won't physically touch her or her mom, but his words will.

A half hour later, she's at our door. We don't need to talk. I give her a hug and bring her inside.

In my room, we get ready for bed and she tells me about some of the kids she's watching.

"There's a new girl who just moved in with her dad. Six years old. I swear, she's going to be the one who makes it. She's going to make robots or something, she's so smart." Faye's voice is deep from worry, but she forces it to be light. "I want her to make it, I really do."

She then looks at me and tilts her head to the side. "I want you to make it, too."

I open my mouth to ask her more, but she goes to the bathroom to brush her teeth. And by the time she gets out, the moment is gone.

After turning out the lights, I think of Faye, in the bed next to me, hiding. Every time this happens, I wonder if it'll be the last time. If her dad will come to his senses and stop. If her mom will leave. Every time I ask, Faye changes the subject, but I still feel like I should. With the darkness as my cover, I look up at the ceiling and ask, "Are you okay?"

"Sure," she says, also staring up.

"Seriously."

She pauses and sighs. "Every time he gets a new job, Mom gets so excited. Like *this will be it. This will be the one that'll turn him around.* But it never is. And she doesn't see that."

"Yeah. I guess . . . I guess the alternative is thinking it'll *never* get better. And you can't think that."

"Welcome to my world."

"Faye . . ."

"It's true. I don't think he'll magically get better. I don't think a job can do that. And I sure as hell don't think we make him happy."

"He's your dad," I try. "Despite . . . everything . . ."

"He thinks I'm okay. I'm sure somewhere he likes me, even loves me, but he doesn't care. So it's easier for me not to care, too."

I turn to her. "It sucks you think that way."

She turns to me. "I care about what's important, and about who's important. I care about my mom. And you. And, god, even Logan. I care about those kids."

"I know you do."

She looks away, then looks back. "I want them to know that. So if they're ever in a situation like mine—I mean, I hope they're not, but if they are—they'll know someone cares."

"I wish I could help."

"You do," she says, and in the dark I see her sadly smile. Then she turns over to fall asleep.

She never talks so much about her situation, and it pains me to hear. It's been years like this, I've gotten used to it, and every time I feel so utterly helpless. I wish I could do something, but what's there to do? Other than listen.

It makes me grateful for her, for our friendship. And for my dad. That he's *not* like that. That we're just . . . us.

Again I wonder if Faye could want something different than here, that she could try to change the world in a bigger way outside of our tiny neighborhood. Show all the kids that she cares. So I think of the future, because it's out there, unaware of us speeding toward it.

I think again of Sam and Chase and their infinite possibilities, and what making it means to them. And then I think of Faye, babysitting the same kids and so invested in it. Both paths so different, but both are confident in where they're heading. Sam and Chase are excited to leave and find success. Faye wants to stay here and make a difference in kids' lives. Her path is so much more noble. Her big dreams are just much smaller and more realistic.

I never thought about leaving, that was never an option really, with the restaurant. And I'm okay with that. Because I can make it here, too. With Faye beside me, with us together, I think maybe we have an infinite amount of possibilities here, too. Maybe I just have to look for them.

FIVE

In the morning, Faye leaves when I do. We split ways at the top of the block.

"See you after camp?" I say.

"I'll make time for it." She grins, then adds, "Thanks. Again."

"Anytime."

I get to my acting class with a smile on my face.

"We're going to start with duet acting," Miles says, and I shift in my seat, ready to go. "I know you auditioned to get in, but this will be my personal assessment of your acting ability. Monologues worked fine then, but now I want to see how you work with other actors."

He paces around the room and picks up a pile of scripts. "Partners will be random, and everyone is going to do the same scene for today. With that, we'll be able to see how each person individualizes their character. Essentially how, depending on the actor, one character can be interpreted many different ways. How there's not one perfect way to act. That's what's unique about acting—nothing is right or wrong."

"Isn't there always a right way to do things? Isn't there the way the writer intended?" I mumble to Sam. She shrugs and looks just as confused as me.

"There are more girls than guys," a girl in the back points out. She's tall and pretty, with curly hair and big blue eyes.

"True, which is why there's no gender in this scene. Anyone can be either character. Take that as you will," he says, giving the girl a significant glance.

"Let's redeem ourselves," Sam whispers to me, holding her hand out. I grab it and give her a squeeze. We sit leaning toward each other, hoping Miles will understand.

He starts pointing to people two by two. I fidget in my seat, and look around to see who's left, wondering who my partner might be.

"Right, you," he says, pointing to me. My heart picks up in my chest, and I say, "Penny," and he nods. "Penny, you're with . . ." He assesses who's left and points to . . . "Chase. Chase, you're with Penny."

And deep disappointment hits. Sam elbows me in the side and when I look at her, she's wiggling her eyebrows. I shake my head and sigh.

Chase grabs our scripts and comes over to me. "Guess we're partners?" He grins. I kind of smile back, hoping he won't critique me this whole time, too.

"I guess we are," I say.

◇◇◇◇

About an hour later, we're deep into rehearsing the scene, sitting on two beanbag chairs in the back corner of the room. Our characters are married, we agreed, and are fighting over food. I get what our teacher said; it's a very basic scene that we can do so much with. It's an argument, but a simple one. We can make it more.

"I don't know what you're saying," he says, reading from the script. Chase, for his part, is really good, which annoys me. It just makes his criticisms more, I don't know, valid. But it also pushes me to be better, because I don't want him to show me up.

"I can't believe you left it out!" I yell as best I can. He looks at me for a second, then stops, dropping his character.

"Why did you yell that again?" he asks.

"Because she's angry. Because you're being annoying," I answer.

"Yeah, but did she need to yell it?"

"Yeah. She's angry, so she yells."

"Hmmm," he says, eyeing me. "You're not really good at this, are you?"

I nearly shoot back in my seat. "At what? At acting?"

"You can tell you're new at it. Like, maybe, what, two or three plays in?"

"I've done a few shows. . . ." I say defensively.

"You've got so much room to grow."

"Excuse me?" I glare at him. "Who *are* you?"

He ignores my question. "You're trying too hard. Like, this should be an easy scene. I'm hardly sweating."

"I may not be as natural as you are, but I'm good," I say, pulse rising.

"You're fine, but not good."

I shake my head in disbelief. "I'm. Good."

"You're fine." He waves me away. "I should have been paired with someone else."

"What the . . ." I start, catching myself. I look at him in the face and say, "I'm good. I'm going to show you that I'm good. I'm much better than you think."

His face slowly breaks into a grin. "That's it!"

"What's it?" I nearly shout, exasperated.

"That's perfect. What you just did. Like, you were angry with me, right? And you just slowly reprimanded me. You didn't yell, you didn't go crazy. You just looked at me like you wanted to murder me. That's so much more effective than yelling."

"Wait . . . what?" I ask, confused, then realization dawns on me. "Were you . . . were you messing with me?"

"Oh, totally. You're not awful. I just wanted to piss you

off to show you that you didn't have to yell to get your point across."

I'm absolutely speechless for a moment. "You're such a—"

"Ass? Totally. But one who means well." He grins this stupid cocky grin and I want to punch him in the face. But then I think of the scene.

And he's right.

It would be more effective if I was quiet and deadpan and serious.

It would get the point across so much better. It's like how I saw my dad fire the guy who was stealing silverware at the restaurant—he didn't yell; he was stern. Angry.

I'm not sure how Chase knew, but he did. And he got the performance out of me. Which is frustrating (because he was right again) and exciting (because . . . I did it).

After an hour, we perform for the class. We're fifth and, as it turns out, Chase was right; most other pairs scream the fight scene. They're good, believable, but not entirely convincing. I look at Chase, who's moved his seat next to mine, and he gives me a wink. He's thinking the same thing. So when it's our turn, I feel confident.

"Ready?" Chase whispers as we walk to the front of the classroom.

"Yeah." I smile. We turn to each other, scripts still in hand, and say our lines.

"I don't know what you're saying," he reads, and it's time.

Instead of yelling, I keep my voice low and calculating. "I can't believe you left it out." He stares at me for a beat, and I stare back. The room is silent.

"It was an accident," he continues, and the rest of the scene goes smoothly. I swear, when we're done, Miles smiles.

When we get back to our seats, Chase puts his hand on my shoulder and whispers, "See?"

I nod, realizing how much the moment, the feeling and validation, meant to me. Yeah, Chase, I saw.

◇◇◇◇

After class, Chase finds me during lunch as I walk to an empty table. Most students go out for lunch; I bring mine.

"Come with me," he says, putting his arm around my shoulders and pulling me away.

"What? Where?" I ask, struggling and thinking of my peanut butter and jelly sandwich in my shoulder bag. When he turns me toward the theater, I add, "No food in the theater."

"No food *in* the theater, but no one said anything about *above* it."

I narrow my eyes at him, but curiosity gets to me, and I let him pull me in.

We walk through the empty auditorium, going between rows of seats. "I have a boyfriend," I say quietly, self-consciously. My voice feels like it's echoing through the room.

"Okay," he says. "I wasn't trying to bang you or anything." My face flushes in response.

"I bet people have here. You know, broken in overnight. Climbed up to the catwalk. Which, incidentally, is where we're going."

"The catwalk?" I ask. "We're not light techies. I don't think we can go up there."

"We were never told we couldn't, so I think it's fair game," he says, opening the door to the tech booth at the back of the theater. "Besides, who's going to stop us, the theater police?"

I scowl but, still curious, follow him past the light and sound control boards and to a set of stairs that lead up to the catwalk.

The black metal stairs are a bit rickety, but we make it to the top, where there's a thin platform that juts out above the rest of the auditorium. I look down and my knees buckle from the height.

"I, um," I say.

"You're okay with heights, right." He tells me more than asks. Heart pounding, I look up at his cocked eyebrow and challenge it.

"Yep, fine," I say, straightening out and looking ahead rather than down.

I hold on to the two metal railings on either side and follow him to the center, where the lights are hanging. It's directly over the middle of the theater, rows J, K, L. He sits down, crossing his legs, so I do the same, slowly and carefully, not wanting to fall, and also not wanting to flash him.

My gray skater dress was perhaps not the best outfit for this.

"Now, isn't this better than the cafeteria?" He leans back on the railing and opens a bag of chips.

"It's pretty high up."

"You can see everything from here."

"Have you been up here before?"

"Nope, decided to come today on a whim. You're my first guest, Penelope."

I blush at him saying my name for some reason, maybe it's because it's my full name, my adult name, and not what I've been called my whole life. "It's Penny."

He looks at me. "I like Penelope better."

"Well, I like Penny." He doesn't respond, so I ask, "So do you still hate it here?"

"It's okay. Atlanta is more of a city, you know? Here it's kind of, like, a fake city. Like it's trying hard to be something it's not."

"How is a city trying to be a city?"

"It's trying to be New York, when it's more like . . . I don't know, the South."

"Winter Park is not the South. Georgia is more southern than here."

"Should I show you a map?"

I wave my hand to dismiss him. "You know what I mean. Atlanta is different, but a good part of Georgia is more southern. You know, sweet tea and *y'all*. Like north Florida. Here is, like, metropolitan in comparison."

"So you're saying it's more northern the farther south you go."

"Kind of. But not really. I can't explain it. You should see where I live." As soon as I say it, I regret it.

"You don't live here?"

"A few cities over," I say. "More suburban than here. Picket fences and all that." It's not the entire truth, but it sounds nice. There are fences, and it sounds better than *My best friend lived in a trailer until a year ago.*

"Ah. I'm learning so much about Florida," he says dryly, like he doesn't really care. "So much more than the joke it seems to be."

"It is," I say defensively. I look down again at the theater below us as we sit in awkward silence for a moment.

"So what's this boyfriend of yours doing right now?" Chase asks.

"Working."

"Where's he work?"

"For a rental company. They lease those cool bounce houses for fancy parties, and—"

"Sounds fun," Chase says, yawning. "So, tell me, what's fun to do around here?"

"I don't know, really. Um. Movies? Or Disney. There's always that."

"I think I'm past the mouse days. I want to go out."

I pause. "My friends and I usually just hang out at my house. Sometimes we walk around the mall. There's a dollar theater that has sticky floors and ripped seats, but it's a dollar, so we don't care." I chuckle, but look over at Chase, who is shaking his head. "Well, it's clearly not Atlanta for you," I mumble. He's making me feel nervous, like I might say the wrong thing at any minute. Like I might sound stupid. I probably already do.

"Every city has a downtown area. I'm guessing yours does, too."

"Oh, yeah," I say. "But I haven't really been."

He raises an eyebrow at me. "Why not?"

"Because it's mostly bars, and that's not really my scene." Since I can't exactly get in, but I don't add that. Also, my dad would definitely not like me going.

"We'll remedy that. Might as well explore, right? See what's out there?"

I note the word "we'll" and don't answer.

An awkward silence rolls over us as we sit staring into the theater, so I change the subject to something more familiar. "So why did you audition for here if you plan on doing film and stuff?"

He moves forward and dangles his legs off the catwalk. "I never said I didn't want to do theater. Acting is acting."

"You say that like it's easy."

"Isn't it?" he asks with a sly grin.

"So that was it? You just thought you'd audition and got in?"

"Yeah, why wouldn't I audition? I mean, it's a good camp,

something to do over the summer. . . ."

"You know people work hard to get in here, right?"

"I'm not saying people don't, I'm just saying . . . I don't know. Jeez, you're really putting me on the spot."

"Sorry. Curious, I guess."

He turns to me and I feel his eyes scanning me. "Listen, to you this might be a huge thing. And that's cool. But to me it was just another audition. There's so much out there—this is just one audition on the road to many more."

I've never thought of it like that. . . . I just thought it was important, exciting. I never thought about what's next, that it could only be the beginning.

"Have you been outside of Florida?"

I shake my head no. Truth is, I haven't been out of central Florida, but I don't say that.

"You have to go. There's so much more out there."

"Here's not that bad," I say.

"Sure, it's fine. But why settle when you can see if there's something better?"

The silence of the auditorium seems loud all of a sudden.

We eat our lunch and talk more about camp, but nothing really important. After a bit, he stands up and I follow, quickly glancing at my phone and seeing it's time for class soon. "Friday night. I'll find something more fun than a dollar movie. I'll let you know what's up."

"Okay, sure," I force myself to say, because I don't get him. One minute he's insulting me, the next he's pulling me closer.

I follow him back along the catwalk, down the stairs, and back into the auditorium.

"See ya." He walks out the doors and back into the hall and I'm struck with how strange lunch was. Did we just become friends?

"And, hey," he says, looking back at me. "I have a girlfriend. Or two." He grins and then turns back around, walking with all the self-assurance in the world.

I shake my head, having no idea why he came up to me, why he wanted to have lunch with me, why he wants to hang out with me. Why me?

And why am I kind of happy it *is* me?

I stand up taller and turn around, ready for my next lesson. If he can be that assured in his acting, so can I. What's so different about us, after all?

SIX

When the day is over, I hop on the bus and get off one stop before my usual one, where the diner is. I walk the three blocks, past my old middle school. I hated that school for all the reasons to hate middle school, but mostly because of the bars on the windows. How the windows wouldn't open, no matter how much you tried. Faye and I always hated feeling stuck in there, trapped.

I get my key out of my bag and walk up to the café, knowing it closed at three. Dad cut back hours when he realized people only really came for breakfast and lunch, so it cost more to keep it open later. On Wednesdays, Dad stays late to work on the books, so I figured I'd meet him here. When I open the door, I'm hit by the familiar smell of syrup, fried chicken, and fresh biscuits.

"Dad?" I call out, walking past the wooden tables and display cases with knickknacks from the sixties, when my grandparents opened the café. JFK presidential pin, flyer for the Palm Beach International Music and Art Festival, bandannas. It's a weird theme, considering it's a country place, but I wouldn't want it any other way.

"Kitchen," Dad yells.

I go behind the front counter and through the double doors, and find him hunched over a black binder, with glasses perched on his nose.

"Thought I'd come by and see if you needed help with anything, and if you wanted to grab dinner."

He squeezes the bridge of his nose and says, "Eh, we're okay. I'll just be a few more minutes. How was camp?"

"Great," I say. "I showed them I sorta know what I'm doing."

"That's my girl," he says.

"I'll wait in the break room," I say. I go into the neighboring room, a tiny space that smells of old coffee. I throw my bag on the chair, and turn on the TV. He's been somehow getting free cable here since before I could remember, so I flip through a few channels.

About twenty minutes later, I hear the door open.

"Pen-Pen?"

I turn around and give him a big smile.

"Hey, you all set?"

"Yep," I say, clicking off the TV.

"Oh god, not that show again. You know you're an A student, right?"

"It's *interesting*!" I protest, defending my guilt-worthy binging of *Keeping Up with the Kardashians*. I follow him back into the restaurant, and we walk out the door, him locking it behind us.

"Just don't turn into them."

"What, rich and pretty?"

"You can have all of that without having a TV show and walking around half-naked all the time. If you *ever* walk around half-naked—"

"God, I won't, Dad. At least not in front of you," I joke. He shakes his head, and in the setting sun, I see the bags under his eyes and wrinkles on his forehead. "Bad day at work?"

He takes a deep breath. "Long day," he says. "I walked today—mind walking back home instead of catching the bus?"

"Nah," I say, walking across the gravel lot with him, off our property and onto the road.

"Two people called in sick, then the new chef accidentally added hot sauce into the pancake batter. So everything had to be remade."

"Yikes—I'm sorry."

"Not your fault. Unless you put the hot sauce next to the flour."

"Not that I'm aware of." I shake my head, covering my eyes from the glare of the setting sun. Dad walks on my right, so he's closer to the oncoming traffic on our side street.

"That's one thing your mom was great at. Well, she was great at a lot of things, but handling problems? She was a champ. The hot-sauce fiasco would have been fixed in two seconds."

"Didn't something similar happen once?" I ask, kind of recalling another batter mix-up.

"The sprinkles!" Dad said. "God, you remember that? You poured sprinkles into the pancake batter because you wanted it to be happy, or something. I don't remember."

"Wait, it was *me*?" I ask, surprised.

"Oh yeah. If it was anyone else, they would have been fired." He pauses. "No, that's a lie. Your mom kept everyone."

"So what happened with the sprinkles? Did she have to remake the batter?"

A voice calls from across the street and we look over. The beekeeper Dad gets his honey from waves at us and we wave back. "No, your mom calmly explained to everyone that it was the café's birthday, and she'd decided to celebrate. People started requesting sprinkle pancakes after that."

I smile at the story. "That sounds like her. She made her day count."

He nods solemnly, then asks, "So today was good?"

"Really good. We did our scenes, and I think I impressed the teacher."

"Of course you did. Now they'll have to cast you in the show. When are auditions again?"

"Two weeks."

"Are you prepared?"

I look over at him as we turn onto our block. "Dad, I've been there for two days."

"So are you?"

"Ha-ha," I joke and wipe sweat off my forehead. It feels like a million degrees out. Even the birds have disappeared; not one is making noise.

"What's the first show?"

"*The Glass Menagerie.*"

"I'll have to read it. What role are you going for?"

I love his enthusiasm for acting. He never thought about plays before, but ever since I got into it, he's made an effort. He listens to the soundtracks, sees the movies. I know it's his way of trying to bond with me, and I love it that he tries. "I looked the script up yesterday, and there's definitely a role I want. But . . . there are only two girl roles, so I'm nervous to say the least."

"Need me to run lines or anything?"

"Yeah, maybe this weekend. I really want to get in the show. Sam and I are going to start practicing tomorrow."

"A boy? Is he the one you told me about?"

"Girl," I say. "Yeah, her. But, what if it *were* a boy? Am I still not allowed to talk to boys?"

He laughs. "Pen, if I could have it my way, guys wouldn't

be allowed to be within a fifty-mile radius of you."

I don't mention that we're passing my and Logan's tree. "You should probably tell Logan that."

He shakes his head. "Well, let me know if you need me," he says. He breathes in, but doesn't say anything.

"Yeah?" I ask, raising an eyebrow.

He sighs and shakes his head. "Nothing, sorry."

"Nothing? Tell me," I say, not letting him off that easy.

"Nothing to tell," he says, not meeting my eyes. "Let's get dinner. I'm starved."

"Dad."

"Just . . ." He pauses, then sighs. "Thinking about your mom."

"Oh," I say. "Yeah."

"Yeah," he says.

We keep walking up our block to our house. When we get inside, Dad makes us dinner and we talk more about camp and work, but he doesn't bring Mom up again.

A week goes by, and I find myself hanging out with Sam more, mirroring her excitement for the auditions.

"Who are you auditioning for?" I ask her. We're leaning against the wall in the theater's girls' dressing room. We have free time to practice for our audition, so everyone is kind of everywhere, finding small alcoves to rehearse. The Returners—what we now call those who've been coming to camp for several years—are taking the classrooms, the actual theater, basically everywhere that's great. They're traveling in packs. Us newbies have to find places for ourselves. The dressing room, as it turns out, was empty. The smell of wet sock is probably why.

She looks down and finishes scribbling a star on her purple canvas shoes, then grins and says, "Amanda."

"Awesome," I say, relieved. "I'm going for Laura. I was kind of worried we were going for the same part."

"So if we both get in—which we will," she says with a grin, "I get to be your mom."

I grin, "Should I start calling you 'Mom' now?"

She puts on an old-lady voice and hunches over. "Don't you leave the house wearing that."

I laugh. "Perfect. You're a shoo-in."

She steps out of character and asks, seriously, "Are you nervous?"

"You have no idea," I say. "I mean, I love all of this, but I know I'm not as good as everyone else. Plus, I'm just having fun here. I'm not aiming for Broadway or anything."

She shakes her head. "It's not like that for me. I *want* to do this, you know? It's cool you're just having fun, but I want this to be my future. I know it can be." I frown and she adds, "Don't feel bad. I'm super happy you're here—I mean, you're my sanity through all this—but I just want to prove myself."

"I think getting in proves yourself. Doesn't it?"

"To my friends at school, sure, but not people *here*. I want them to know I'm serious."

"Why wouldn't they?"

She shrugs, tapping her sneakers with her fingers, as if itching to add to the intricate Sharpie drawings on them. It's the first time I've seen her unsure. Yeah, we were nervous when we first had that scene together, but she was still the one pushing forward, the one smiling while I was shaking. And since then she's been like a beacon of hope and optimism. I wonder what brought this on. Maybe the fear of auditioning?

Footsteps sound down the hallway and then the door opens. A girl looks in, and then narrows her eyes. "Oh, sorry, didn't know the room was taken."

"Oh, hey, Kate!" Sam says with a wave.

"Samantha," Kate says with a smirk, and then turns around to the other girl she came with, letting the door shut without saying anything else. They both have brightly dyed hot pink hair, and that's all I can think of until I hear the murmuring through the thin walls: "Like she'll even get a role." Then laughter.

My face heats up and my eyes widen as I glance at Sam. Her head is down.

"Who are they?" I ask.

"Girls from my school. Regulars, too. Kate still hates me for getting her role in *Into the Woods* last year. She wanted to be a stepsister, and instead she didn't get cast. At all."

"She's mean enough to be an evil stepsister."

Sam looks at me, then laughs. Really laughs. And I do,

too, until tears are springing from our eyes. And it feels good, like we both let out something we've been holding in.

"Honestly, she's kind of crap," Sam says in a whisper, and adds, "AND her dad totally bought her into this school."

"Really?!"

"Totally. Heard she botched her audition, too." I gasp and think of Faye. Faye would like Sam.

"What did you do for audition?"

"'There's a Fine, Fine Line' from *Avenue Q*. With a puppet."

"*Seriously?* You auditioned with a puppet?"

"Why not?" she asks and I smile.

"I love that. That's going to be my new motto. *Why not?*"

"Why not rehearse? Let's show them," Sam says, picking up her script. There are several scenes where our two characters interact, so we start at the beginning.

And just like that, I can feel something starting. Like we were meant to become friends, and cheer each other on. Because when she acts, I can feel the want and need in her voice. I know it's there. And I find myself wanting to be better. For me.

We go over the scene three times. Once to get used to the dialogue. The second time to further analyze what we're doing. And the third to work on things we critique in each other. Like she needs to take it down a few notches. And I need to take it up.

"Are you sure?" I ask, feeling a bit conflicted. I'm never

great when it comes to critiques.

"Penny, yes. Laura's shy, but I have to be able to hear you."

"But she's so meek."

"But your voice isn't. And behind her meekness, she wants."

She wants.

The Glass Menagerie is about a mom, daughter, and son. The father sailed away to adventure and never came back. The son is on the cusp of that, too, but he won't admit it. And the daughter is quiet, stemming from her embarrassment over a leg injury.

Sam continues, "You've got shy, protected, and anxious all worked out. You're all those things. Just show me that she doesn't always want to feel that way."

"But doesn't she?" I flip through the script, having read it a few times already. I wanted the role of Laura because I understood shy and scared and content with life around her. But maybe Sam's right. Maybe in her life she does want more.

And I'm not sure how that makes me feel. About the character of Laura.

Or about me.

After rehearsing, I walk toward the bus stop and see Chase standing at the corner, looking to cross the road. As if he hears me, he turns around and looks at me over his sunglasses. I breathe in as he approaches.

"Riddle me this—how are we supposed to get any rehearsing done if there's no actual place to rehearse?"

"Where'd you end up?" I ask.

"The catwalk."

Of course. "And you didn't get in trouble?"

"Nah," he says, shaking his head. "We were quiet."

I can only assume what that means. I must make a face, because he says, "*Rehearsing.* Quiet rehearsing. Get your head out of the gutter, Penelope."

"It's Penny, not—"

"What about you?" He cuts me off.

"Sam and I were in the girls' dressing room."

"I should have thought about that," he muses. "How'd it go?"

"Good! Good," I say, trying to sound convincing.

"Are you going for *The Glass Menagerie*?"

"Yeah. I'm more of an actor than a singer."

"Same," he says, and I think it's the first time he kind of sort of admitted he might not be perfect at something. "It's a great play to show range for an actor, too. Like, it's pretty intense."

"I know, I'm excited," I say, thinking back to what Sam said, about how I have to play Laura up more. The push to do that is making me more driven now. I really want it.

Chase takes off his sunglasses. "You know, you remind me of a girl from my old school in Atlanta. It's been annoying me."

"How so?"

"She's perky like you. Eager."

"Eager?"

"To act. It's a good thing." He pauses. "She also used to steal my Legos when we were kids."

"That's . . . weird."

"Yeah. Isn't that weird how one thing could forever remind you of someone? Like, she'll always be known as a Lego thief to me."

And you'll be known as the guy who insulted me the first day we met, I think, but instead, I say, "So I remind you of a Lego thief. I'm pretty sure that's insulting."

"Not that part. Just the—ugh, never mind." He shakes his head. "You're confusing me, Penelope."

"Again, Penny, not Penelope—"

"Where are you off to?" he interrupts again.

"Home," I say. "You?"

He shakes his head. "I'm going to Java Jump," he says, thumb pointing across the street where some of the Returners are waving at him.

"You have a fan club," I say.

"They're all right. Where's yours?"

"Oh, you mean my posse? Took the day off. You know, following me around is hard work," I joke.

He smirks. "You are adorable."

There's a shout from the other side of the street, and that girl who insulted Sam is there waving at Chase. "Guess

I'm off," he says. "See you tomorrow. Catwalk lunch?"

"Sure," I say. "Tomorrow." I turn around and walk away from the corner and back to the bus stop, what he said still buzzing in my head. I feel like Java Jump and the Returners are on one side, and Sam and I are on the other. Those girls aren't adorable; they're hot. Those girls aren't café workers—heck, they probably wouldn't even come to our café. They're able to afford fancy coffees. And I'm fine with that, but every time I talk to Chase I wonder . . . what *is* on that other side?

◇◇◇◇

On the bus home, I take out my phone and text Faye.

I was called adorable.

That's because you are. Like a tiny widdle bunny.

I'm never letting you live down the fact that you said widdle.

I'll take one for the team. Who said you're adorable?

Guy in camp. It's nothing. How are you?

Currently covered in glitter. Like, it's everywhere.

I smile. She hasn't brought up her dad since the night she slept over, and I don't want to ask. She knows when to talk to me.

70

Now that's adorable.

BYE.

Question. Is it crazy to act? Like, crazy to do this instead of work with my dad?

I think acting is a million times better than having syrup constantly spilled on you. I mean, for you. For me, I'd take the syrup.

But do you think it'll lead to anything?

Are you having a mid–high school crisis or something? It's just camp.

No! Maybe?

I can practically hear her sighing.

I think you should be happy. And if acting makes you happy, do it.

Even if I'm not trying to go pro?

If you go pro, that means you leave me. So do it here and NEVER LEAVE ME EVER.

Promise. I'm just more into getting this role than I thought I'd be.

That's because you finally realize you're GOOD. That's a compliment, by the way. You know those don't come easy from me.

<3

I love Faye for so many reasons, but mostly because she always knows how to say the right thing when I need to hear it.

When the bus stops, I don't feel like going straight home, so I walk to Logan's. It's been a few days since I've seen him last, and we've almost never gone *days* without seeing each other.

The thing is, being apart is starting to feel normal, and that's . . . different. I don't know how I feel about it. Because I miss constantly being with him, but on the other hand, I'm kinda enjoying camp on my own.

I knock on the door, and when he answers, his whole face lights up.

"Hi." I giggle when I walk in, hugging him.

"Too long," he says into my hair. "I was about to start making out with a pillow."

"Isn't that how you learned to kiss?" I joke, pulling away, and he rolls his eyes.

"At least it was a hot pillow."

"Penny?" His mom pokes her head out of the kitchen. "I thought I heard your voice. Nice to see you. I feel like it's been years." She walks out of the kitchen. Her red hair is up in a bun, and she's wearing a pink-and-white-striped apron. She's a baker at a wedding cake shop, one of the two owners. The store does okay; everyone always needs a cake. When she's not coming up with new designs, she's making muffins or cookies for Logan and his baseball team. "How are you, dear?" she asks, taking me in her arms.

"I'm good, thanks."

"How's camp? Logan says you're auditioning for a show soon?"

"Next Monday, yeah," I say, nodding, a bit nervous he told her. I didn't tell anyone I was auditioning for my first play, just in case I didn't get it. I didn't want that look of *Oh, sorry, you failed.*

"Well, let me know how it goes. You were so good in your last show. I know Logan loves watching you act."

"Mom," he says.

"Thanks." I blush.

"So what are you two up to today?" she asks, wiping her hands on her apron.

"She just got here, so I don't know." Logan shrugs. "Watching Mikey. Hanging out. Nothing really."

"Well, when you're done doing nothing, I have cupcakes that need tasting."

"Done," I say with a smile.

She goes back to the kitchen and gets us two pink-and-white cupcakes. "Sugar cookie flavor," she says. "Have fun!"

"Can I live here?" I ask Logan as soon as his mom leaves.

"Only if you sleep in my room," he answers as he pulls me to him. Just as I sink onto his bed, "DOOR OPEN" is yelled from the other room. I laugh and Logan sighs, opening the door wider. "We never should have told her about us."

"Hey, you were the one who did. You wanted to be 'honest,'" I say, making air quotes.

"Just so she wouldn't wonder why we're always together."

"We've been inseparable since we were seven. We clearly weren't dating then."

"Honestly, she probably thought we were. She told me the other day that we're the 'perfect' couple, and I'm like, *Okay, thanks, Mom, gross.*"

"Yeah, your mom's love for us is a bit much," I say, feeling comfortable. I needed this—a jump back to what I know, what I'm used to. I needed time with him.

"But let's be honest," Logan says, and then drops on the bed next to me, both of us leaning up against the wall. "This whole door-open thing is ridiculous. It's not like we're going to do anything while she's, like, five steps away."

"Or are we?" I look at him with an eyebrow raised, and he shakes his head.

"Don't tempt me."

I kiss him quickly on the lips, then dig into the cupcake.

"Oh, this is really good. Like, *really* good." I take another bite and feel the frosting all over my mouth.

"You've got something . . ." Logan says, then leans over and kisses my mouth right where the frosting is.

"Door open," his mom calls, and we spring apart quickly, faces equally red. When we realize she's not literally looking into the room, we both laugh awkwardly.

"Let's sneak away," he says, a chuckle in his voice.

As he says it, a little ball of energy runs into the room. "LOGAN, COME HELP ME MAKE LEGO CASTLE!" Mikey, his little brother, is a tiny, six-year-old force, and he's my favorite thing, aside from Logan himself.

"Okay, okay, let's go." I smile as Logan is pulled from the bed into Mikey's room just next door, connected to his with a shared bathroom. I follow behind and watch them build, not even concerned that Mikey didn't notice me. To him, I'm this girl who's been around his whole life. Logan, however, is his hero.

"Like my tower?" Logan asks, pointing to a row of balancing blocks on the head of a Batman figure.

"You're so talented." I shake my head and join in, handing more blocks. And it all feels so natural.

"Okay, I'm leaving," his mom says from the door a little later. "Delivering a cake to a retirement party," she explains, and then looks fully at the scene around her—the three of us nearly ankle-deep in blocks creating a very high tower. "I'm so lucky to have such great kids. All of you," she says, looking pointedly at me. I blush again, knowing she's considered me her third kid for a long time. But since Logan and I started dating, it's felt different. And now, knowing what she said about us, maybe a bit awkward.

I twist a yellow Lego in my hand and think of Chase, and what he said earlier about the girl from home, the Lego thief, and how one thing can define a whole person. Mikey would be defined by his eternal energy. He's the same every time I see him. And Logan? That first time we met, with the baseball. Yeah, I guess that would be it.

"Hey," I ask Logan. "If you could remember me by one thing, what would it be?"

"That's a morbid question," he says, screwing a wheel onto a block car.

"No, not in a dead way, but in a . . . just . . . What reminds you of me?"

He's lying on his stomach, and turns to me. "What brings this up?"

"ICE POPS!" Mikey yells. We both turn to him. "I want ice pops."

I smile and turn back to Logan. "Like that—general enthusiasm about everything reminds me of Mikey."

"I think that's every six-year-old," Logan says.

"Come on." I lie down next to him on my stomach and nudge his shoulder.

"Okay, okay. I don't know . . . Theater, obviously. Bangs, because they cover up like ninety percent of your face." He flips my bangs and I swat at his hand. "Baseball, because that's how we met."

"That's what I was thinking." I smile.

"And humming. Because you do it when you're happy."

I hum the Batman theme at him for his, and Mikey's, pleasure.

We continue building into the night. Mikey babbling the whole time. Logan beside me, occasionally slipping me a glance. And in the midst of it all, I think about how Logan knows me. I don't need to be defined by one moment, he just gets me. Chase may have his side of the road, but I'm just fine here.

SEVEN

We pile into the auditorium on Monday morning, everyone 100 percent more awake than normal. The smell of coffee wafts through the room, as the Returners pass cups of it among them and whisper behind one another's backs. I huddle next to Sam in the second row.

"So I reread my part, like, seventeen times," she says, staring at the stage.

"This weekend?"

"This morning."

Teresa walks onstage and instantly everyone is quiet. After a few announcements, she gets to auditions. "Okay, everybody listen up. Auditions are all day today, here in the auditorium. Times are being posted right now outside the doors, as well as outside our other rooms. Be patient; be respectful. These are professional auditions, so do not be late. On time is late. Please check for your time . . . and make us proud."

I hold my breath and script at the same time. Despite practicing all week with Sam, and over the weekend with Dad, I'm still insanely nervous. Sam is next to me . . . smiling, as if what comes next is the most exciting thing in the world. Like we're at the top of the roller coaster and she's thrilled for the decline and I'm scared to death. Scared I won't be good enough. Scared I'll freeze up and not do anything. And . . . scared of how much I want this.

"While you're not auditioning," Teresa continues, "feel free to practice around campus. This is a free day in terms of lessons, but don't just sit around. You won't get anywhere just sitting around. Okay. Break a leg."

With that, she claps three times and pushes herself off the stage. I file out with Sam, wiping my sweating hands on my vintage-looking brown dress. I chose it because it's similar to what other actors have worn while playing Laura.

We get to the front and scramble with everyone else to see the posted times for the two plays. It's a mess of people, so I not-so-patiently wait, all the while twisting my hands in front of me.

"Our sheet's here!" Sam yells, and lines her finger down the paper until she sees her name. I do the same.

"When's your audition?" I ask her.

"Oh, second," she says, a look of shock on her face.

"I'm in an hour." I sigh in relief, then realize her shock. "But you're going to do great, honest." We walk away from the crowd, toward the outside.

"You too! Gosh, okay, I'm going to go over my lines one more time while I wait."

"Need help?"

"No! I'm good. Go walk your nerves out. You are literally shaking," she says.

"I'm fine! I'm fine," I lie.

"You've got this, Penny. You're going to do great! Break a leg!" She grabs me in a hug and then takes off to the water fountain. I head out and into the other building, trying to steady myself.

The hallway is lined with chairs, and everyone is waiting for their time. Crumpled papers shuffle in hands. Some people, like that girl Kate who made fun of Sam, sit high, backs straight and determined looks on their faces. But from the way Kate's breathing—fast and deep—I can tell even she's nervous. I look around and there are about twenty people here, mostly girls, more than likely all out for the same part as me. I look down at my script, then at them. One girl I don't know even dressed in a full period costume. I look down and back up in another direction, not wanting to make eye contact, or else she'll see how much that makes me worried. A guy is leaning back and laughing, not worried at all. The girl with big curly hair from my rotation is staring at me with daggers in her blue eyes, like I'm competition. I turn and walk away.

I feel my phone buzz and pull it out. I have two messages.

> Break a leg, nerd. And let me know if I have to break legs if they get your role.

I shake my head at Faye's message. It's the perfect good-luck message. The next is from Logan.

> Love you. Good luck today.

A hand grabs my arm and twists me around. "Hey, hey, getting ready?"

"Chase," I say as I see his smug face in front of me. I put my phone away and look back at him. He looks so sure, so confident. And I'm . . . a bundle of nerves despite the texts.

"Where ya going?"

"Nowhere," I say, trying to break away. He lets go but continues to look at me. "I was thinking of getting fresh air. Going outside."

"Isn't your slot this hour? I highly recommend staying. They might be running early. And from what I hear, every-one kind of sucks so far."

"They *just* started. No one can suck so far," I say. "Besides, how would you know, anyway?"

"I have my ways." He grins.

"I'm sure you do." I look at the hall of people, then back to him. "When are you?"

"Later today, in two hours."

"Are you nervous?"

"Nah, I've done harder auditions," he says flippantly, and I shake my head.

"Not helping."

"What? Don't tell me you are."

"Why wouldn't I be?"

He shrugs. "Because it's just an audition for a play."

I glare at him. "It means something to me, okay?"

He raises his hands in protest. "Okay, okay. I wasn't saying it didn't." He looks at me for a second, then looks down. "Okay, sorry. I can be—"

"Obnoxious?"

"Confident," he corrects me. "Obnoxious?" I shrug in agreement. "Let's go practice."

"Didn't you just say I shouldn't leave because of my audition time?" I challenge him.

"We're not leaving." And with that he pulls me down the hall and into a tiny classroom with about ten desks in a circle. "You're frustrating, you know that, right?"

"What?" I gasp, then realize what he's doing. "No, don't do this again. I'm not falling for your fake insulting me, just to make me perform better. Just tell me what I should do and I'll consider it."

He crosses his arms. "I'm not faking it. I don't think you realize how good you are."

"Uh-huh." I copy his pose, crossing my arms.

"No, seriously. You're, like, the only competition I have in class. You're that good."

That's . . . not what I was expecting him to say. "Really?"

"Yeah. I'm attracted to talent. I'm not gonna hang out with just anyone."

I roll my eyes. "What about Kate and company? Are they talented?"

"No, they're just hot." He grins and I shake my head.

"So you're hanging out with me because I'm talented," I repeat.

"Yeah. So stop being scared, and go kick ass at your audition." I purse my lips and stay quiet. Because what do I say to that? I think I'm good, sure, but not that good, I guess. Not Chase level. And I didn't think he thought that of me. "Listen, I directed at my old school. I was kind of shitty at it, because I didn't listen to what the actors thought, only what *I* thought. They let me know before I left."

"Okay."

"I want to direct, like, after everything. I want to act, but I want to direct. So I'm trying this whole listening-to-people thing."

"You're doing a great job," I say dryly.

"Just freaking practice. Go. Practice so you're not nervous. I want to act with good actors, and you're a good actor."

"Ah, so it is for selfish reasons," I say, but I smile. Because despite his words, I believe him. I am good.

He sighs in response and sits on one of the desks. I sit next to him. "Sorry, I'm not used to people taking so much interest in my acting. Okay, that came out pathetic. My friends are supportive and I love that, but in school, I'm never the lead or anything. And I know I'm good, but I guess . . . I'm surprised you think so, too."

"You know, most girls would take a compliment and run. Not you."

"I'm stubborn."

"I like it," he says, raising an eyebrow. "Feel calmer now?"

"Y-yeah," I say, soft. He's close, really close. We're too close. I shake my head, breathe in, and sit down. Clear my head.

Chase clears his voice and says, "Let's run your scene."

"Okay," I say, and for some reason, Logan comes to mind. How he doesn't push me like this, not anymore. If I say I don't want to do something, or go somewhere, he's fine with it. And I like that about him. He's simple. When I decided to quit chorus, favoring drama, he said, "Sounds good." If he'd pushed me, would I have stayed?

I don't need a guy to push me to do something. I can do what I want.

Still, I think of what he said this morning, on the phone, before I left. "You're gonna get this; you know you will. It's meant for you." He only knew so much about the play—what I told him—but I think he'd say that about any role I went for. Anything that would make me happy. He's just that nice.

And while that makes me happy, for some reason Chase saying I'm talented makes me feel even better. Confident. Logan *has* to say I'm good because I'm his girlfriend; Chase doesn't. Logan makes me feel comforted, but Chase gives me hope.

Which is probably why I nod and take out my script.

"Well," I say. "I'm not throwing away my shot," I say with a wink, quoting the musical *Hamilton*.

Chase moans and says, "Let's go." He plays opposite me, not the role he's going for, but the one other guy role. We run the scene twice, once to get out my nerves, the second to perfect it. And each time it gets better. I start to separate his criticisms from having a mean intent to being helpful. They give me something to work for, to do. To be better.

By the end I feel more comfortable, confident, and in control of the character. I feel more like her. Maybe Sam was right in her assessment. The character, Laura, is happy how she is—in her tiny, protected world. But maybe she *does* want more. I use that thought as I leave the room. And when I get to the audition, I do exactly what Chase says. I look at them with all the hope and determination in my small body. I let them know they can trust me, that I'm perfect for the role.

That it's meant to be.

And when I start the scene, I'm not just acting. I believe it, too.

EIGHT

"Oh my gosh!"

"What?" Faye answers. "What's wrong? What's going on?"

"The audition! I just got out!" I yell into the phone as I walk to the bus.

"Jesus, Pen, I thought it was an emergency. Don't scare me like that."

"Ahh, sorry, sorry, I'm just excited!"

"So I guess it went well?"

"Really well. I'm coming over."

I jump on the bus and watch as the city disappears, replaced by country, the high-rises becoming small houses. And the feeling of being onstage diminishes into the feeling of being . . . just me.

I knock on Faye's door and her father answers, a gruff, large man wearing a stained white tank top. He looks at me and yells out, "Faye," before returning to his chair in front of the TV.

"Hey," she says, walking to the door and grabbing my arm. "Walk with me."

I turn around as she pulls me, then slams the door behind us without a good-bye.

"Sorry," she says when we're a few houses down. "Rough day. He's decided that I'm going to work even more hours this summer to support him while he takes time off."

"Why'd he lose his job again?" I ask.

"Why do you think? It was a construction job and he complained to the owner about being in the sun too long. It's a freaking construction job; of course you're in the sun too long."

"What'd your mom say?"

She sighs. "She feels bad for him, like always. Like he's the victim. She's just . . . ugh, she doesn't get it for some reason. He's such a deadbeat."

"I'm sorry," I say, not sure what else *to* say.

She waves her hand. "It's the usual. I just hate it." She pauses. "Promise me you won't get like that with Logan. All *He's a perfect angel who never does anything wrong.* Because they all do something wrong eventually."

"I promise," I say, but I can't think of anything Logan *does* do wrong intentionally. "Where are we going, by the way?"

"I don't know. Just out. I wanted to get away."

"You're not working now?"

"Nope, off today. Hey, let's go get some ice cream or something. You can tell me all about *l'école de théâtre*."

"You remember so much more from French class than I do."

"I literally only remember the word for acting school because you said it so often. *Oh, the acting school will be so great. Oh, the acting school will be so professional.*"

"Hush," I say and grin because that takes me back to when I found out I was accepted, and it seemed like a world of possibility and wonder. And it still kind of is.

We walk to the Ice Cream Shack, a small storefront that has really cheap ice cream that you order from the outdoor counter. It's nothing special—nothing like those places that mix in cake batter and strawberries, but it's one dollar, so you really can't complain. After getting Faye's chocolate and my strawberry, we sit on the wooden benches. The sun's already melting our ice cream, so we eat fast, finding words between our gulps.

"So the audition went well?"

"You don't want to talk more about your dad?" I ask. "Because—"

"Nope, done. I mean, what else is there to say? So, your turn," she says quickly.

"Okay." I pause. "Well, yeah, it went really well. Better than I thought."

"That's awesome. When do you find out if you got the part?"

"A few days. There're callbacks first, so . . ."

She takes one last bite of her ice cream and tosses her napkin into the garbage. A bird standing watch jumps and flies away. "So it's going well, yeah? The whole camp thing?"

"Yeah," I say. "It's cool. Everyone's really good and it's intimidating, but fun, I think."

"You think?"

I tilt my head and say, "I mean, it *is* fun. But sometimes getting told you can do better over and over again starts to get exhausting."

"See, that's why I wouldn't last there. I'd yell at everyone."

"I'd love to see that," I say, smiling.

"How're your new friends, who are in no way as cool as me?"

"Ha," I say. "No one can replace you!" I tug on her hair.

"You know it."

"This girl Sam, I think you'd like her. She's stubborn, like you."

"Hey, I am more than just stubborn."

"And nice?"

"I'll take it."

"Sam's super confident. Everyone is, really. They all want to go on and do amazing things. You know, go to New York or L.A., become real actors."

"Don't tell me you're going to get all Hollywood now, too."

"Nah." I pause, then give the same answer I tell everyone. "I'm not leaving. I'm not risking everything on a wild dream. Not my style. I've got enough here."

"Exactly. Like me."

I lick my ice cream as it drips down onto my hand, onto the table. "I know you're staying, too, but have you ever thought about leaving? I mean, going somewhere else after high school?"

She shakes her head. "I can't afford it. Even if I magically get a scholarship—which we both know won't happen with my grades—there's no way I can afford a place to live somewhere else." She shrugs. "I just want to get out of my parents' house eventually. Get a job, and get out."

"And you're okay staying here after next year?"

"You're not?" she asks, raising her eyebrow.

"No, I am," I say quickly. "I have you and Logan and my dad. I have the café. I like it here. I just . . . I don't know. I guess I never considered leaving."

"Okay, consider it right now. This second. Think about leaving. What do you feel?"

I look up at the sky and see the birds flying overhead, going somewhere. Moving on. Leaving. I could do that, too. I could leave. But do I want to? I think of the café, and Dad. I think of Mom and the hopes she had for me. And I think of Logan and Faye right next to me. I'd be stupid to give it all up.

"I feel scared," I admit. "Scared of not knowing what'll happen next."

"And what do you feel when you think about being here?"

"Safe," I say. There's no pressure. There's no fear. It's just . . . safe.

But is safe what I want?

We're not far from the bounce-house place, so we decide to drop in on Logan. He's working the register when we walk in and talking to an older woman who's inquiring about princess-themed bounce houses.

"And it has Elsa, right? We need Elsa on it." She has a thick southern accent and a full skirt—the picture of a southern belle. Faye rolls her eyes.

"It has Elsa on it," he assures her, pointing to a picture in a book. This must be one of the moms he's been complaining about. He's cut his hair shorter since I saw him last, but it's still puffing out around the ears, making him look so imperfect and cute.

"Okay, good. Because it's a themed party. Elsa's going to be there. My Sadie is very excited."

"I'm sure she'll love this," he says, scratching his head. He looks up and when his eyes catch mine, I swear his face lightens. Since the woman is looking down at her phone, he nods at her and rolls his eyes. I smile and signal for him to take his time. In the meantime, Faye and I wait by the door. She grabs one of the brochures and flips through.

"Oh, I call pirate ship," she whispers, pointing to the pirate-themed bounce house, which also has a slide that goes into a blow-up pool.

"Yessss," I whisper back. "Oh, or how about clown? That's not terrifying or anything," I say, pointing to one with a bunch of creepy, happy clown faces painted on it.

Faye shivers, and I laugh. My phone vibrates, and I look to see I have a message from my dad.

How'd auditions go?

GREAT! Excited to tell you all about it later.

After responding to him and checking my email, I look up and see Logan hop over the front counter.

"Whoa," I say, as he crouches in front of me. I lean down and give him a quick kiss, my heart thumping with happiness at seeing him.

"I was excited," he says, smiling at me.

"Hi, I'm here, too," Faye says.

"Awww, come here," he says, opening his arms and making a kissing face. I giggle and Faye shakes her head.

"No. Gross."

Logan looks back at me and nods to the desk. "I thought she'd never leave."

"Well, she was very specific about what she wanted. . . ."

"They're all like that. Especially when it comes to Elsa."

"Let it go, Logan, let it go," Faye says, and we both roll our eyes at her reference to the song. "You have zero idea how many times I'm still forced to hear that song. And it's like a million years old."

"Okay, you win," I say. "How's your day going?" I turn back to Logan and ask.

He shrugs. "Fine, a lot of this." He stands up and sits on the chair next to me. "I prefer days when we're actually out setting them up at parties. At least we're doing something. I feel like I'm totally out of practice."

"In inflating them?" I ask, confused.

"No, with baseball. My only practice has been with Mikey, and we haven't really had a lot of time to get drills in."

"I love that you do drills with your brother." I smile.

"He takes after me," he says, just as a girl walks in. She's tall and thin with a face full of makeup. She looks a little older than us, maybe college. Both her shorts and shirt are really tiny. She looks around, then back at us.

"Oh, hey, Logan," she says, then sees us. "Am I interrupting?"

"No, it's okay," he says, standing up, looking professional. "What's going on?"

"Brad needs you outside," she says, and I can't help but wonder who she is. Does she work here, too?

"Cool, coming," he says. As he follows her out, he holds up one finger and mouths *One second* to me.

When the door shuts, Faye says, "I hate her."

"Seriously." I don't really *hate* her, but I am jealous of her height. And beauty. And ease at, I don't know, walking.

"I bet she wakes up like that, too. With, like, birds flying through her window to help her get ready."

I poke her in the side. "Is all this talk about Elsa bringing out the inner princess in you?"

"If I haven't turned into a princess in all the times I've *played* princess with the girls on my block, there's no way I'll magically transform now."

"Darn. I really wanted to see you in a poufy dress." I hear some yelling and look behind me out the window.

Faye follows my line of vision to see an inflatable pirate ship. "Oh, we should totally try out one of the bounce houses!"

"I don't think we can just go bounce on them."

"They probably need a tester, right? Let's go."

"Sometimes I think I should be babysitting you." I shake my head.

"Look, one's all set up," she says, ignoring me and walking toward the door. "Let's just look at it. Touch it." I look at her begging eyes and sigh, nodding in agreement. We can't get in trouble for just looking.

We head back outside and I see Logan standing next to the girl and Brad. They're talking and laughing, and it's weird standing on the side seeing him with them. Not that I'm not used to him hanging out with other people—he has the entire baseball team, but I just *know* all of them. I don't know this girl.

I guess that might be how he'd be if he saw me talking to Sam. Or Chase. Thinking of him reminds me of the moment we shared before rehearsing and I have to mentally stop my cheeks from burning.

I turn around to see Faye standing in front of a castle. Her hands are at her waist, balled in fists, and she's leaning back, looking at the top.

"My parents would never have gotten me this," she says. "But how cool would it be to get one for the neighborhood? God, the kids would freak."

"They'd love it," I agree.

"You think I could sneak it out? Fit it in my pocket?"

"Of course." I laugh. "I think that's entirely possible."

She turns around and sits on the side. "Oooh, comfy."

"Do you think we should—"

"Come on, I'm just sitting on it."

I turn around and join her sitting on the hot yellow plastic. It *is* comfy.

She bounces a little, then says, kind of dreamily, "Yeah, this would be perfect."

"HEY," a voice calls out, jolting us both. We look over and it's the tall, pretty girl waving her hands at us. "You can't sit on that."

We pop up and Faye rolls her eyes. "We weren't doing anything," she says under her breath. But I'm nervous; I don't want to get Logan in trouble.

"What're you guys doing?" Logan says, running over to us.

"Stealing your bounce house!" Faye says, and I shake my head.

"We were just sitting on the side, nothing big," I say.

"You can't do that," he says. "It's against rules . . . and you can get hurt."

"If people could get hurt *sitting* on these things, you probably shouldn't be renting them," Faye says.

Logan ignores her, looking only at me. "Some aren't completely blown up. And they could break."

"Sorry, we didn't know," I say, feeling bad. Especially when I see Her walking in our direction.

"I could get in trouble," he whispers.

"I know, I know, I'm sorry," I say, looking at him, then Faye. She nods along.

"You guys can't be over here," the girl says, and my face heats up.

Logan responds, "Pen, this is Sally, the owner's daughter. Sally, Penny and Faye."

"Hi," I say, a little embarrassed.

"Ah, Penny the actress. I've heard about you," she says.

I kind of stare at her for a minute, not sure what to say. What do you say to that? And then Faye interrupts.

"Hey, Sally, is it? Can I talk to you about a charitable opportunity?" She waves her over and walks back to the bounce house, explaining about her job.

"She seems nice," I say, turning to Logan.

"She's okay." He shrugs.

"Look, I'm really sorry about before. I don't want to get you in trouble. I know what this job means for you."

"It's okay," he says. "No damage done. I just, you know, get worried. I can't lose this job."

"Yeah, I understand."

He brushes my hair away from my face and says, "Day's done anyway. Walk home?"

"Yeah," I say, "that would be great."

◇◇◇◇

We drop Faye off back at her house, and then walk to my house.

"I just can't get the hang of it," he says, referring to the different knots used to tie down the houses. "I know half of them, but there are a lot. I feel like a sailor or something."

"But it's not all bad, right? The job?" I ask.

"Eh, it's okay. I mean, it's not what I'm going to do the rest of my life, so I don't care. The money is okay, and Mom's happy." I smile at him, thinking about how he's doing all this for just his mom. Making sure she has money to pay bills and support him and his brother when her bakery isn't doing well. It makes me love him even more. I've seen them in every stage, from pre–dad leaving to post–when life was chaotic, and he's always been the rock for the family. We used to shut ourselves in a closet with Mikey so he wouldn't hear their mom crying. We'd hold flashlights and tell loud stories that were supposed to be scary, but were mostly funny. Once, Mikey laughed so hard it stopped the crying outside.

"You're great," I say.

"You're just saying that."

"I mean, maybe." I smile and rub my nose against his.

We keep walking and he slows down in front of a *For Sale* sign on a house at the edge of my block. He furrows his face and asks, "Someone's moving?"

"I don't know," I say, shaking my head. An older couple lives there. They used to give apples instead of candy when we went trick-or-treating. They always kind of creeped me out, but as they got older it was worse. They were like that big black haunted mansion at the end of the block you never went to, but instead of a scary house, they lived in a one-story, two-bedroom home.

I look at him and as I see his face scrunch, I know we're thinking the same thing. People don't always move from here. People leave, but not by choice. People die.

People like my mom.

"Do you think—" I start, but he cuts me off.

"Let's go home."

I tear my eyes away from the house and follow him down the street in silence. Then he says, "It's okay. It might not be—"

"It is," I say, knowing it's true. Feeling sad not just for their loss, but for the loss in general. For the lack of permanence. How everything ends. For my mom's body on the side of the road, thrown from her car. For the fact that *things happen* and we can't control them.

Did the couple always want to live like that, handing out apples instead of candy? Did they always want to be the recluses on the edge of a block? Is that their legacy? Did Mom always want to be here, at the restaurant, or could she have gotten out before it was too late?

We head into my house and up to my room. Maybe it's fear, or the belief that tomorrow isn't promised, but I manage to say, "I want more." And only when the words come out do I realize they're true.

Logan says, "Okay," but I know he doesn't get it because instead of asking, *What do you want?* he kisses my head, my nose, my mouth. He kisses me to make me forget, to make me feel better. To make me believe that it'll all be okay.

But will it? People change. People die. It happens. And it's out of our control.

But I kiss him back, to do something. Because I need to do something. He's on me, hands in my hair, and I feel it— the rush, the panic, the intensity. The want for this to never end. The fear that it might. I hold on tighter, grip harder, with the knowledge that this moment, despite everything, is ours.

We break apart for a second, and his brown eyes bore into mine. "I love you," he says.

"I love you, too," I say, and I know I do.

But I don't know if love is enough.

NINE

The next morning, I'm woken by a commotion outside my room. Something falls. Some choice words are said.

I rub my eyes. "Dad?" I ask, opening my door.

"Sorry!" he calls from the kitchen. "Dropped the coffee-maker."

"How'd you drop the coffeemaker?" I croak, entering the kitchen and seeing him cleaning up a mess on the floor. I get a paper towel and join him.

"I put it on the counter, close to the edge, and . . . never mind, go back to bed, it's early."

I yawn, then throw away the wet paper towel. "I'm up now."

"Sorry." He shakes his head. "How were auditions? I didn't see you last night. . . ."

"Oh, right! I'd almost forgotten that was yesterday. Great, really. Callback list will be posted today."

"You'll be on it," he says with conviction.

I smile and sit at the kitchen table as he straightens up and tries making coffee again. "Let's not get ahead of ourselves."

"You're great. Tell me the results as soon as possible."

"I will." Something hits me, and I jerk up. "Wait, where *were* you last night? That long getting things shut down?"

"Ah, no," he says, a worry line creasing his forehead. "Just out with the guys. Needed a night out—you know how it is."

"Tsk, tsk. Out past your curfew," I joke. "Where'd you go?"

"Just a bar, nothing exciting," he says quickly, turning around.

"Who went?" I ask.

"Just friends." He shrugs, not looking back at me. He's been doing this more and more lately: going out, not giving me details. Definitely hiding something. Or someone. Did he have a date?

"You're being kinda mysterious. Anyone special?"

"Not really. But, hey, I have to go. Short on staff this morning." He turns back around and gives me his classic everything-is-okay dad smile.

"Okay," I say. He messes my hair, then walks out of the room.

It's still another hour until I have to get ready to leave for camp, so I lean back, then rethink and head back to my room and pick up Mom's notebook. For some reason it's calling me. I know I won't find all the answers in there, but holding it makes her feel closer to me. I flip through the pages again and feel her handwriting, feel the pressure she put on each word. How it makes each word feel important, like it's worthy of her touch.

I really wish she were here with me right now.

◇◇◇◇

When I get to camp, the entrance to the theater is eerily empty and I quickly realize the callback list must be posted. I walk in and once I open the doors, a loud chatter echoing off the walls replaces the silence I heard outside.

My heart skips a beat as I run in and see everyone piled up against the auditorium doors. Heart racing, eyes wide, I squeeze my fists in anticipation, and head on into the crowd.

I maneuver my way around people and feel an arm slide over my shoulders. I look and Chase is holding on to me.

"Let's look," he says. I don't even have time to register the familiar motion; I just turn back around and see the page.

CALLBACK LIST: The Glass Menagerie
Callbacks will be tomorrow in the auditorium.

AMANDA: Tori Brice, Samantha Myers, Reina Sawyer
TOM: Kieran Brown, Dashiell Saire, Chase Matthews
LAURA: Lea Brown, Gabby Forman, Penelope Nelson
GENTLEMAN CALLER: Jarrod Johnson, Micah Weisman, Jackson Wilks

"Oh my gosh, I made it!" I squeal and instinctively hug Chase, pulling him in tight. He reacts, hugging me back, his chin on my head, a familiar move that Logan usually does. Logan. I pull away a little too quickly.

"So did I," he says, smiling.

"I'm so excited!" I say, happiness overflowing. "And Sam made it, too!"

We squeeze back through the wall of people, looking for Sam as I move. She's not here. Still, I get out my phone and text her.

Callbacks up! Where are you?!

"All right, all right, class time," I hear Teresa yell to scoot us all out to our first lessons.

"Ugh, class," I say to Chase.

"Yeah, I'll be right there," he replies, but he's preoccupied with a girl whose arms have slid around his waist. I think of Logan, and his arms around me, and how warm and comfortable it feels. I should text him.

Got a callback!! Next audition tomorrow. Eee!

While waiting for his response, I text Faye.

CALLBACK!

BOOM. You are an acting QUEEN.

I laugh and put my phone in my bag. I'll check for Logan's response once I get to class. On the way, I stop in the bathroom.

When I open the door, I hear sniffling coming from the stall farthest from the door. I go into another stall and look down. A purple messenger bag is on the floor. Next to it, purple canvas sneakers with Sharpie scribbles all over them.

Sam.

I knock on the wall. "Sam? Hey, it's Penny."

"Penny?" she says, her voice cracking.

"You okay? Class is starting."

I hear the stall door click open, so I quickly grab my bag and get out of mine. She's sitting on the floor leaning against the wall.

"Hey, what's wrong?" I ask gently, sitting down next to her. "I saw you got a callback for Amanda. That's amazing. I knew you would."

"Yeah, thanks," she says, playing with the hem of her jeans. "*I'm* happy I got the callback. But not everyone is."

"Oh," I say. "Kate?"

"She's just talking crap about me. About how I don't deserve it and all."

"That's *so* not true!" I say. "You totally deserve it. You worked as hard as anyone else. You won this callback."

"I know, but she doesn't see it that way. She just sees me getting in her way. Maybe it would be different if I looked like her, if I were beautiful like her."

"Um, you're beautiful," I say, trying to cheer her up, but not knowing what to say. At all. I feel helpless.

"I know I'm bigger; it's not a surprise. I just hoped . . . I didn't think it would affect roles I'd get. I mean, I know I can't be, like, a stripper or something. But . . ."

"Sam, that *doesn't* matter. Not here. They're casting based on talent. And even if they were based on looks, I think you look great. Plus, you're, like, the most optimistic person I know."

She looks at me and grabs my hand. "You're delusional, but thank you."

"Kate's just jealous because you're competition."

She nods her head. "I know. She totally is. Let's be honest—she's good, but she's not as good as me."

"That's the Sam I know."

She unties her sneakers and reties them, playing with the laces. "The thing is, I like my body. I like how I look. I just hate how she makes me feel about it."

"Who cares what she thinks or says?"

Sam smiles, then says, "I saw you were called back. You deserve it, too."

"Thanks."

"And with Chase, no less. I saw you talking to him." She wiggles her eyebrows. "Only the hottest guy here."

"It's not like that," I say, waving my hand. "I have a boyfriend."

"Uh-huh. And is he hot like Chase?"

I think of Logan and smile. "He's my best friend."

"Then can I have Chase?"

I laugh and think that's *exactly* what she needs. A distraction. "He's all yours. Actually, let's have lunch with him today. I think he can help your audition."

"How so?"

"He helped mine." I shrug.

"I don't need a guy to help me. But I'll make an exception for Chase," she says with a wink.

I roll my eyes. "Of course you would." I think of practicing for our audition again, and bite my lip.

"What? What's that face?" she asks.

"Huh? Nothing!"

"Tell me."

"Nothing! He helped me rehearse before my audition. That's it."

"I *knew* it." She points at me.

"It's nothing!" I nearly shout, but she's laughing, and really, that's worth it. "Ugh, I give up with you."

"You love me," she says, resting her head on my shoulder, and I think of Faye. They do remind me of each other, but in different ways. They're both strong and stubborn, but also . . . sensitive. Faye's become hardened about it, and Sam hasn't yet. I don't want her to. "You're really talented. Don't let anyone tell you otherwise."

"I know. And I realize that sounds totally arrogant, but I have to know or I'd never try."

"Then keep knowing," I say, and give her a hug.

◇◇◇◇

After a morning of classes, where everyone mostly just wants to talk about the callback list, I find Sam and drag her to the auditorium.

"What's going on?" she asks. "Pretty sure the cafeteria is that way."

"Did you bring your lunch?"

"Yeah?" she answers, as a question.

"Great, we're eating somewhere else," I say, raising my eyebrows suspiciously.

"Where, the auditorium?"

"Nope." I shake my head, then start walking again, feeling her behind me. "Above it."

I take her the route Chase took me, through the rows of seats and into the control booth.

"Are we going to get in trouble?" she whispers, looking all around us at the light and sound boards.

"I don't know." I shrug.

"Since when did you become a daredevil?"

"I have my secrets." I grin. I point to the stairs to the catwalk and she glares at me.

"That looks so unsafe." But then she smiles and grabs hold. Just then, the door slams. We both turn around.

"Fancy meeting you here," Chase says.

"Oh, Chase, hi," Sam says, letting go of the stairs and quickly putting her hands behind her back.

"Don't worry, I told him to meet us here. And he told me about this," I tell her.

We climb up the small stairs, moving along the catwalk until the three of us are high above the theater, holding on to the metal rails, and standing in a row—Chase, Sam, me. We look like a movie poster, maybe. I feel the cool railing on my hand, and hold on tight.

"What do you think it's like? Performing down there?" Sam asks, nodding at the stage.

"Amazing," I say. "My high school's stage is about a quarter of the size. And the auditorium holds, I don't know, fifty people?"

"Mine has a stage that size, but probably only holds about two hundred in the audience. This can hold, what, five hundred people?" Sam says.

"Think of Broadway," Chase says. "This is only a student theater. Nowhere near Broadway standards."

"You want to do Broadway?" Sam asks, the eagerness back in her voice.

"I want to do film, but I wouldn't say no to Broadway."

I feel my phone buzz and jump, then grab on tight to the railing. "Whoops," I laugh nervously. I take out my phone.

Will be home late. Order pizza for dinner! On me.

This is the second night in a row my dad's come home late, and third night in the past week. It's getting frustrating, but I'm afraid he goes out to forget the problems at the restaurant, so I don't want to ask.

"All okay?" Sam asks, sensing my discomfort, I guess.

"Oh, yeah," I say. "My dad's just going to be late tonight."

"Party at your house," Chase says.

"I don't think so."

"So, Chase," Sam interjects, "what's your favorite show?"

"Like, play?" he asks, and she nods. "Probably . . . *Cyrano de Bergerac*. I did a scene from it last year. I used a sword."

"Nice," Sam says. "Penny?"

"I'll say *RENT*. Do musicals count?"

"Totally, and yes. Amazing. Mine is *Les Mis*, of course."

"Dream role?" I ask.

"Did this turn into twenty questions or something?" Chase asks, crossing his arms and looking at us.

Sam smiles. "We don't know you well enough yet, so this is us getting to know you."

"And judge you," I add with the most innocent look.

"I see," he says. "I don't know. Probably Romeo or something. I'd use a sword."

"I'm sensing you like swords," I say.

"Mine's definitely Sally Bowles from *Cabaret*. Her songs! I die," Sam says.

"I don't know mine!" I say. "Okay, honestly, probably Velma in *Chicago*."

"Scandalous!" Sam says. "A husband-killing prisoner barely wearing clothes. I like it."

"That's not why!" I say, but part of me kind of does like that part. I mean, not the murdering part. "Well, I guess, kind of. I haven't played a character so opposite me, and I think I'd like to. You know, it's a chance to be someone completely different."

"I get that," Sam says. "Is that why you like acting?"

I look out at the theater. "I never really thought *why* I liked acting; I just do. I guess. I like living all these different lives. Pretending I'm someone else every now and then."

"See, this is why you need to get out more," Chase says. "You can pretend that in real life. Like, go to a party, use a fake name. Boom."

"Is this something you do?" Sam asks with a wry smile.

"Sometimes." He shrugs. "It's fun," he says.

"So if not for the pretend aspect, why do you act?" I ask Chase.

"I like the feeling," he says. "You feel important, invincible when you're up there." He nods to the stage. "Like you're in charge."

"Are you not in charge of your own life?" I ask.

"Nah, I am, but this is different. . . ."

He drifts off, and I want to ask more, but he doesn't look like he wants to answer. So, instead, I turn to Sam. "What about you?"

"I guess a mixture," she says. "I like the attention. I like that I'm good at it. I like that people see I'm good at something."

I nod and realize we all act for different reasons. They're all valid and important. We all need acting for ourselves. To feel seen, to feel important, to feel . . . unique.

Sam looks down from the catwalk. "That will be me. Up there on the stage one day. I can see it."

"I know," I say, and give her a hug. Then I turn around, thinking I can maybe see myself there, too.

◇◇◇◇

I head to Faye's after camp. She texted to let me know she's just outside playing, so I figured she wouldn't mind the company. And I don't really want to go to an empty house right now. I really should talk to my dad.

When I get to her street, Faye is sitting on the ground, decorating the sidewalk with chalk along with two of the girls she babysits for. They're about four or five. Everyone is wearing tiaras.

"Your Highnesses," I say, looking down.

Faye looks up and her mouth twists into a sly smile. "Queen Penny. As you can see, the royals have come to play.

What, dear, shall we help you with?"

"Hush," I say, sitting down next to her. She gives me a piece of chalk.

"What are we drawing?" I ask, looking around.

"We're making our perfect kingdom," Faye says, finishing up a dragon in a tutu, next to a puppy and a flower. "Young squires," she says, looking down at the kids. "I think a royal game of hopscotch is in order!"

"Yay!" they yell, and the two girls walk a few feet down and start drawing a hopscotch board.

"Thought I'd get us a few minutes to talk," Faye says, wiping her chalky hands on her T-shirt. "So, I got that bounce-house lady to make me a deal."

"Really?! How?" I ask.

"End of summer she'll bring a bounce house here as a charity thing, but only if she can advertise and get a few birthday parties out of it. She won't get any parties, obviously—no one can afford her rates—but I don't have to say that. She'll bring one here. For free. For the kids."

"That's *amazing*. How did you do that? She didn't look like the generous type."

"Everyone has a price, Penny."

"And hers was?"

"Making her feel ridiculously bad about herself, comparing her life to these kids'."

"You make it sound like the kids are little orphan vagrants here."

"It's not my fault if my words are a bit more exaggerated than they should be."

"You're ridiculous." I shake my head, smiling.

"And awesome. And queen of a bouncy castle!"

I laugh. "Congratulations, Your Majesty. That's really going to be awesome. I'll be there."

"You'd better be. I'll need your boyfriend to set it up, I'm sure." She goes back to drawing, then asks, "How're things?"

"Things are okay," I say, then, since it's on my mind, "Actually, my dad's been out a lot lately. Missing dinners. And it always seems like he wants to tell me something, but doesn't finish his sentence. Like the words are on the tip of his tongue, but he swallows them instead."

"That's weird. Your dad is always so open with you."

"Yeah," I agree. "I don't know."

"Do you think he met someone? That would totally explain him being out."

"I was thinking that." I nod. "And then I stopped because . . ."

"You don't want to think about your dad making out with someone. Yeah, I get that."

"Right. Gross. Thanks for the visual, by the way."

"Anytime." She sticks out her tongue at me, in a make-out way, and I nudge her arm. "What about you? How's . . ."

"My dad is whatever, if that's what you're asking. Same with Mom."

"I was going to call and check on you, but . . ."

"But you remembered that phones aren't my thing?" She cuts me off with a smile.

"Pretty much. You know, one day we're going to be away from each other in college, and I'm going to call you all the time, just to annoy you."

She looks up and cocks her head. "How far away are you planning to be? Aren't we both set for school here?"

I jolt for a second because she's right. She's right and I forgot. "Yeah! Yeah of course, but, you know, if we're not in the same apartment or something . . ."

"Which we probably won't be, since you'll go to the fancy university, and I'll go to community college."

"First off, you know I'm planning on going to community college. There's no way I can afford the university."

"You will. You've got the grades, the plans. You know what you want to do. You'll get a scholarship or something." She stretches out on the concrete, resting back on her elbows.

"I'm not that sure."

"Whatever," Faye says. "You've had your life planned out since you were, like, two. You were a toddler talking about the financial stability of the restaurant."

"I was *really* advanced," I joke. "Anyway, you can totally get into the university if you want to."

"Yeah, with my grades," she snorts, "they'll be aching to have me."

"We can get past that. And you can get a scholarship!

Like, a work-while-learning one!"

"I love your optimism." I think of Sam, happy her enthusiasm rubbed off on me.

"You can get one, based on . . . you know . . . needs, too."

She nods her head. "Yeah, about that. My dad told me I needed to take on another kid. Because I wasn't making him enough money as is."

"What? That's ridiculous."

"I know. But . . ."

"But you did it, and now you have zero time to yourself."

"Pretty much. New kid is nice, though. Single dad raises her. Young, only four."

"You're an angel."

"In black. And with horns. I don't do those wings," she says, and I smile. "Actually, that's her dad right now." A man dressed in a blue suit comes out of his car and walks into his house.

One of the girls runs up and curtsies to me. "I'm Princess Emily of Horseyville."

"Hello, Princess Emily of Horseyville."

The other girl joins and says, "And I'm Knight Amanda of Horseyville."

I laugh. "Hello, Knight Amanda of Horseyville. I'm, um, Queen Penelope of, um, this corner."

The kids laugh and Princess Emily says, "This corner?"

Faye answers, "Queen Penelope is not very creative.

Also, since when were you Penelope?"

"I don't know," I say, realizing I said it, and thinking of Chase. He still calls me that. And I still correct him. "Sounds more regal."

"I want to be a brave knight when I grow up," Knight Amanda says, pointing her toy sword and piece of chalk up in the air. "What do you want to be?"

"Oh, ummm . . ." The words hit me in a way I never expected them to. After today's conversation in the theater, and just talking about college with Faye . . . it all seems so . . . weird and relevant. I should know this, shouldn't I? I can't exactly explain that I plan on settling down and that makes me happy. I want to act. But what do I want to be?

"BUTTERFLY," Princess Emily screams and we all jump. The two girls go off chasing after the butterfly and giggling.

I turn to Faye, who's cleaning up the chalk. "Hey, Faye. What do you want to be when you grow up?"

Without even looking up she answers, "A princess with a big fluffy pony."

"No, really."

"Are we in fifth grade again? Should I make a vision board about this?" She looks at me and sees that I'm not joking. "You know I want to be a teacher; that hasn't changed."

"Okay. Cool." I nod.

"Why are you so preoccupied with the future lately?"

"I don't know," I admit. "I feel like we're asked what we want to be, like, all the time when we're kids, and later, when it's actually important and, like, tangible, no one asks anymore."

"They do. They ask what electives you want in school. They ask what you want to major in."

"I took art as an elective, and that doesn't mean I want to be an artist."

"Touché," she says. "Maybe it's because they assume we know. By now we've had time to figure it out. And if we haven't yet, we will and shouldn't be pressured."

"You've known what you wanted to be since you were a baby."

"Same with you." She points to me.

"What do I want to be?" I ask her.

"I mean, I don't know exactly, but you want to work in the café. Be a manager? You want to manage and become a famous local actress."

I pause, repeating what she said in my mind. Is that it? Is that what I give up? I mean, it's true, it is, but I also want so much more.

Faye closes the chalk box and shifts. "Hey, Penny."

"Yeah?"

"What do you want to be when you grow up?"

I look at her and answer, "I really don't know."

TEN

The next day I show up for callbacks and everything feels different. They're harder than the audition, more intense, and when I leave I don't feel nearly as confident as I did earlier. Instead of going out with Logan, I head home and mindlessly watch TV until my eyes don't want to stay open, trying to ignore the weary look Teresa gave me as I did the final monologue, the feeling in the pit of my stomach. It took my mind off how easy Chase seemed to have it, practically lounging through his scenes, and how my hands shook as I acted.

So two days later, on Friday, I know the cast list is posted because it's silent outside again.

I open the door and see the mass of people squished against the wall and my heart jumps. Everyone wants to know who's cast in the two shows. It feels surreal, as if everything around me is made of waves, knowing I'm one of the select few to see if I have a lead.

Like a magnet pulling me, I walk straight ahead, ducking around people. I know some eyes are on me, but I just keep walking until I get there.

I breathe in, then look at the cast list for *The Glass Menagerie*. And there's my name, fourth down.

LAURA, UNDERSTUDY: Penelope Nelson

Understudy.

A range of emotions sweeps over me, and I'm not sure which to grab on to. Excitement over seeing my name on a cast list. Disappointment that I didn't get the role. Happiness that I *am* the understudy, meaning I still get to learn the role and perform it at least once. Sadness that I'll *only* perform it once. But still, pride over the fact that I did it. *I did it.*

I back up to let others through, trying to feel happier than I am. I wonder who else was cast and quickly look back. I don't know the girl who got my role, only from the audition really, but I guess I will. And Chase, of course, is cast as Tom, the male lead. His arrogance paid off. Or maybe he really is that talented.

And Sam. Sam got the role of Amanda. My heart soars for her, and I turn around to see if she's nearby.

"Penny!" a woman's voice calls. I whip around. Teresa waves me over and I follow her. We go through the side doors, past the dressing rooms, and into a small room in the hall. It's not really an office, more like a room with two desks haphazardly placed inside, and I guess that's where she and Miles work. There are books overflowing on a bookcase, and papers all over their desks.

"A few things," she says. "First off, I saw on your application that you've done props for shows before."

"Yeah!" I say eagerly, shaking off my previous funk. I can't look disappointed to her. "I loved working props, finding the perfect pieces needed for a scene."

"Wonderful! Would you be interested in helping out with it here? We need someone, and I thought I'd ask you. You don't have to, of course—"

"No! I'd love to!" I answer quickly.

"Great," she says, and hands me a piece of paper. "Here's a list of all the things you'll need to procure. You'll be using department funds, of course. Also, go through all of the items we already own and the ones that the school owns, as we're allowed to use those, to see if you can reuse anything. Frugality is key here."

"Okay, I can do that," I say, nodding and thinking of the secondhand dress I'm wearing that was three sizes too big originally. A little bit of altering and it fits perfectly. All for about five dollars.

"Great. Don't worry about set pieces, just the small things. Most important Laura's glass collection. As you know, in the script Laura collects tiny glass animals. I trust you'll find them."

"Yes, definitely," I say, nodding my head. Getting excited to start my quest, despite having zero idea where to find everything.

"Speaking of, I wanted to congratulate you on your understudy role."

"Thank you." I somewhat smile, still unsure how I feel about it all.

"Your audition was tremendous—we were all very impressed."

"Thank you so much," I say again, this time really smiling, but also wondering—if it was so good, why not the role?

"Penny, do you know why I cast you as the understudy?" she asks, as if reading my mind.

"No?"

She sits down and places her chin in her hands. "You're . . . you're like a new painting. A few strokes on the canvas, that's all, and we're not sure where you're going. Will you be a flower? A house? A skyline?" I must look confused, because she shakes her head and says, "Anyway, you're good, very good, and I know you'll handle the role exceptionally well. But before we give you such a difficult, major role, I want you to be a little more experienced. I want you to know

123

which direction you're going."

I nod my head and think back to my conversation with Faye. Where am I going? What do I want to do? I still don't know. "So I should be more like a finished painting?" I ask, going back to the analogy.

"Finished? No. Partway there, yes, but not finished. Never finished. When you're finished, you have nothing left to learn."

I leave her office with those words in my mind. I shouldn't be finished, but I should be more sure. I should know what I want, why I'm here. *Am* I here just to have fun? Or am I here because I want something more? I didn't think personal problems could affect a role—I didn't realize we can't always separate.

When I turn the corner, I see Sam waiting for me. I instinctively smile.

"SAM!" I yell, throwing my arms around her. "Congratulations!"

"You too!" She says, jumping up and down and giving me a big hug. When we break apart, we grin, and for the first time today I let the real excitement filter through me. "I can't believe I got it. I mean, the competition was *fierce*, and I was fine, but there are so many other people who could have gotten the role. And, like, I'm new here. And, oh my gosh, I'm so excited."

I grin as she babbles because it's the first time since auditions that she's sounded like that same bubbly, optimistic, overenthusiastic person I first met. And it's nice hearing that again.

"And you!" she says.

"Thanks." I smile. "I'm excited. It'll be fun and not as, you know, stressful for me," I say, waving my hand, down-playing my disappointment.

"We should celebrate this weekend!"

"Yes! We should!"

"Did I hear 'celebrate'?" I turn and see Chase walking toward us, seemingly five feet taller than he actually is. It's the ego, I'm sure.

"Hey, congratulations!" I say, pumping my fists in the air. He grabs my arms and pulls me to him, enveloping me in a hug. His chest is hard, like Logan's, and I break away, thinking of him.

"You too," he says, looking at me.

"This is going to be so much fun!" I whip around and see Sam dancing in excitement and I smile.

"What do you say? Party this weekend?" Chase asks, still looking at me.

"Um, yeah, sure," I say, looking back at him. I get this twisted feeling in my stomach that's part excitement and part apprehension. Because I know Logan would feel weird about it.

"Hey, Chase, congratulations," Kate says, gently slipping her arm over his shoulders. I want to say something, but I see Sam's eyes narrow and instead go to her.

"Yeah, thanks." He grins, wrapping his arm around her waist. Then he turns with her and walks in the other direction before looking back. "Party this weekend."

I nod. "Didn't you say he has a girlfriend?" Sam asks, watching them leave.

"I think he has a few," I say, shaking my head. He's confusing; he really is.

◇◇◇◇

I see Logan waiting for me at the bus stop.

"I knew you'd get it!" He cheers when I get off the bus, hands around his mouth to mimic a microphone.

I smile and run up to him, wrapping myself in his arms. "You say that because you have to."

"I say that because I believe in you."

"Awwwwwww." I step away and take his hand as we walk back to my house. "So what's on the agenda for this weekend?"

"Well, I'm working tonight."

"No!" I whine. "You said we'd celebrate!"

"You know I'd love to, but it's a summer graduation party, or something, and they wanted a rental, and . . ."

"I know, I know, but I feel like you're always working at night," I complain.

"We can hang out tomorrow. Maybe Faye's free tonight?"

"No way. She's never free Friday nights. That's when a lot of the parents go out."

"That must suck."

I shrug. "She doesn't seem to mind it."

"At least she likes her job."

I pull on his arm to get him to stop. "I thought you said it was okay?"

"It's fine and all, just not what I want to do. More like what I have to do. Like with your acting, I wish I could do that, you know? Something fun."

"Is there something with baseball you can do instead? Volunteer with a camp to coach or something like that?"

"Nah. Those things don't pay. I need to help Mom get by. She needs me."

"She needs your dad's child support."

Logan grinds his teeth, then looks away.

"Sorry. I just mean it shouldn't all be on you."

"Yeah, but it is. And there's nothing to do about it." He sounds harsh and hopeless. I should remember to not bring up his father.

We walk in the direction of the woods, the only noises surrounding us are car engines, lawn mowers, cicadas, and the occasional bird's tweet.

We get to our spot, the fallen log, and sit down silently side by side. Only a few weeks have passed, but for some reason we already feel different—like doing two different things over the summer is already pulling us apart. I lace my arm through his and lean my head on his shoulder.

"Mom's bakery isn't doing too well right now. I mean, it's fine; it's not going to close or anything, but it's not at, like, the prime it once was. So I feel . . . like . . . I have to help out, so she doesn't stress. So we can keep going the way we were. Just in case, you know? And I don't want Mikey to know, of course."

"Do you think he does?"

"No. I mean, I think he knows we're not as rich as some of his friends. Like, we don't take summer vacations and most of his clothes were mine. But he doesn't ask about it. He just goes along with it all."

I nod. "I was like that. I never asked, either."

"Once my dad left, I was a pain about it, I'm sure. I was older, but I still didn't get why I couldn't go to the movies with friends all the time, why things had to change," he says, leaning his elbows on his knees. "Complaining why I couldn't get these cool sneakers and stuff."

"You were frustrated; you didn't know any better."

He looks at me. "You did. As a kid."

I shrug. "I don't know how. I just knew not to ask. I remember my parents talking about money a lot. And I remember my mom looking at the price of a doll once and sighing and, I guess, I got it then."

"Yeah, well, when my dad was around we had some money, so I didn't experience all this, you know? But then Dad started drinking. . . ."

I remember it well. I guess maybe he'd always drank, but it became more frequent, more obvious. Always a can in his hand. "Have you talked to him?" I ask gently.

"Not . . . lately. He texted me last week, something about coming to visit. But he doesn't ever call. He doesn't actually talk to us. So why would we want to talk to him? Why would we even want to visit him after what he did to Mom?"

"Did to all of you."

"Yeah . . ."

"I guess if he texted, that's good. Is he . . . getting better?"

"God, no." He shakes his head. "He left the woman he left my mom for. Did I tell you?"

"No! What happened?"

Logan shrugs again. "Who knows. It's like . . . He was married to my mom for years, then left her for this woman. And then left her for another one, and I'm sure he's on another one now. He's acting like the guys at school who go after every cheerleader, when he's, like, a *dad*. It's so weird."

"I don't know how you deal with it," I admit. "Put up with that."

"Well, you know."

"Yeah, I know," I say, thinking of how he takes out his anger on the baseball field. Thinking of the bucket of balls he hit the one time his dad forgot his birthday.

He exhales. "Thanks."

"For what?"

"You know," he says, nudging my foot with his.

"I'm always here for you; you know that."

"I know," he says, looking down. I instinctively rub my hand through his hair, and he shivers. "Promise me something. Promise me you won't leave. Like my dad, you won't just leave."

I nod, but I don't feel 100 percent as sure of that as I did a few weeks ago. There's more out there, and I can see it. But I can't tell that to Logan. And it worries me that I'm unsure.

I push the thoughts from my head and rest on his shoulder, feeling the comfort of the familiar movement, and breathe in the smell of trees and grass and sweat. It feels like all the summers before, but just a little different. The log we're sitting on is rough, digging into my legs, and I wonder if it always felt like this.

"I promise," I say.

ELEVEN

I go home feeling weary, restless, off. It's like the excitement of today was transferred into this unease about everything. I want to get my mind off things, so I text Faye, even though I know she's working.

Babysitting tonight?

Obv. New girl. Dad is out on a date or something ooooohhhhhhh.

"Ohhhh" is right. Logan's busy, too. I wanted to celebrate.

Yeah! Excited?

Really.

This is your thing.

I think about that—it's my thing. It's what I'm known for. All the shows I'm in, all the plays I've made her see. I love that it's my thing.

Which reminds me. A mom I babysit for teaches at the community college and told me about a play she went to there. They have a theater program. You should do it.

This isn't really new news—I knew about it, I'd looked it up before. It's good, not great. But it's something. And the fact that she looked into it for me means a lot.

I think I will. Still be acting that way, right?

Yep. And I'll still be forced to watch.

UGH YOU.

KIDDING.

I still want to celebrate, BTW.

Don't go too crazy. Lunch tomorrow? My treat.

Your treat? I'm getting everything on the menu.

Invitation canceled.

I laugh, and then see one more text from her.

Congratulations again. You're awesome.

Thank you.

I click off my phone and then flop on my bed, disappointed but smiling. Dad's still not home. Even he has a life tonight.

After Mom, we were both kind of hermits, slowly moving, but not quite leaving. I left the house for the first time a month later. It took him two. I don't know who these new friends of his are, but I'm glad he has them. Still, I want to know more. I'm still worried.

But if Dad's going out, I don't want to sit here by myself. I feel antsy, like I need to move.

Maybe Sam's free?

I grab my phone and see I have a text from Chase.

Celebrate?

I look up at the door and listen to the emptiness outside. I look back down and type.

Pick me up?

Sure. Where?

Just as I'm about to type my address, I hear a shot in the distance and jump. Running to the window, I remember the season, remember what's going on. It's gator hunting. Every year around now, people are free to hunt down the gators that pollute our lakes and retention ponds. It's an odd event and inhumane . . . and I don't want Chase seeing or hearing all of that. He knows me as the girl from a fancy camp. He doesn't need to know I live in a tiny house with trailers nearby. I don't want his opinion of me to change. So I text back "the library" and link him to the address.

I walk a few blocks up the street to the library. It's just getting dark, so I'm a little wary. My neighborhood is fine but there've been some incidents recently—a burglary at a shop down the street, a carjacking at the car wash. I look both ways constantly. I keep my hands in my pockets, clutching my keys in case I need them. I don't make eye contact with anyone walking, either.

The library is open and bright and loud inside. At least, loud for a library. There's a musician playing acoustic guitar, and people sitting in front of him, kind of bopping their heads. A bunch of people are walking around the shelves, pulling out DVDs and books. I didn't know it was such a popular place on a Friday night. I should probably come here more often.

I wander the aisles and find the theater section. They don't have many plays, but they have enough for me to flip through as I wait, small paperbacks all stacked together. A few familiar ones, some not so much. One for *The Glass Menagerie*. I pick up a very worn copy of *The Collected Shorter Plays* by Samuel Beckett at random. We read *Waiting for Godot* in English class this past year. I didn't really like it, but my teacher was so passionate about it that I kind of appreciated it. I flip through, nothing really catching my eye, until I get to the final page.

Perhaps my best years are gone. When there was a chance of happiness. But I wouldn't want them back. Not with the fire in me now. No, I wouldn't want them back.

I read it again. And again. I'm not sure if it makes me happy or sad. The guy seems to have left all that makes him happy, but he has passion now, and maybe that's a good thing. Something new? And maybe going back would take all that away from him?

I like the sentiment.

I feel my phone buzz in my pocket.

Where are you?

I put the book back on the shelf and walk outside. I don't see him, just a bunch of parked cars. So I start to text him back.

"This is a weird place to meet."

I jump and turn around to see him behind me.

"You scared me!"

"I try. What's going on?"

"Nothing," I say, calming myself down. "Thanks for picking me up."

"No problem." He shrugs. "Some people from school are going to downtown Orlando. I thought maybe you'd want to meet up."

I find myself nodding and wondering who from school. I've never hung out there before. There are clubs and bars and I don't drink, so I never cared to go, but maybe it could be fun. A feeling of apprehension of going out with Chase alone, of going downtown in general, washes over me, but I push it aside.

"You ready? Or do you need to read or something?" he asks jokingly.

"Funny. Let's go," I say.

I follow him to his shiny, new car. When I sit down, the apprehension comes back. I'm in a car with Chase, a guy I only kind of know. We're about to go downtown. My friends

aren't here with me. It feels new and different, and I don't
know what to think. So I text Sam, because I need to tell
someone.

> **Going downtown with Chase.**

> WHAT? Details.

> **Don't know! I have no details—it just happened. Come with?**

> This is so mysterious. Let me know where you're going, and I'll see if
> I can leave. Ooooh, you're with Chase!

> **Still not like that.**

> Uh-huh.

I hide my smile and look out the window at the dark-
ened streets.

"So you live around here?" Chase asks. "Is it really called
Christmas? That's what the GPS said."

"Yep," I say.

"Does Santa live here?"

I roll my eyes. "You know how unoriginal that is, right?"

"Yes." He laughs, and I smile to myself.

Chase takes off down the interstate and rolls the windows down. A warm, balmy breeze rushes in. The cars cruise

past, the buildings blurring by, all taking me farther from where I started. Chase drives fast, faster than he should, probably, but I don't care. I should be scared, but I'm not. The downtown skyline comes into view, and I sigh. It's not large and majestic like the pictures of New York I've seen, but it's ours and still a little bit magical, I guess.

I lean out the window just a little bit and take in the night, closing my eyes. I let the wind push me and pull me and twist me around until I may take flight, too.

"What're you doing?"

"Huh?" I ask, jolted back to the present. "Sorry, just feeling the breeze. It's been hot."

"It's always hot."

"Yeah."

He's quiet, then says, "That's one thing Atlanta has that's better—skyline. Yours is so small here."

"It's not that bad. It's still tall."

"Tall? You need to get out more often. This is nothing."

"Well, it's not New York," I say.

"That's for sure."

More silence. I've never been in such close quarters with Chase. Usually, we're at school around other people, or on the catwalk with the theater all around us. Here, it's just us in a car, and it's like the closeness has stifled our conversation. Maybe we don't work like this. I think of Logan, and remember I didn't tell him where I'm going. Not that I have to, but it still feels like I'm sneaking out.

Actually, I didn't tell my dad, either. I send him a quick message.

Going out with friends. Be home before curfew.

A few minutes pass, and I don't hear back from him. Hmmm.

"Have you been downtown before?" I ask Chase to make conversation.

"Last weekend," he says, tapping his fingers on the steering wheel. "With some of the others from camp. You know, Lea, Kate, Dashiell. We'll see them tonight."

"Oh, cool," I say, instantly regretting inviting Sam since Kate will be there. "Where'd you go?"

"Saw a band at Sapphire."

"Good show?"

"Eh, it was fine," he says. "We explored after, and that was awesome. We found this statue that's, like, half underground. It's a woman's head and arms coming out from the ground. You know it?"

"No! Where is it?"

"By the lake. It's totally creepy. Took some pictures with it. Oh, and we found this, like, musical wall."

"Huh?"

"By the library. This wall with, like, handprints that you press and they make music."

"That can't be real," I say.

"Totally is."

"Were you drinking?" I ask jokingly.

"Yeah," he says, laughing. "But that doesn't mean it didn't happen."

"Well, please show me this magical wall."

"Oh, I will."

I look at him and wonder why he invited me tonight. Why not just go out with them? Why bring me along? I don't know how to ask that, so I settle with "Sorry I missed it last time. Thanks for bringing me tonight."

"It's cool," he says, glancing at me quickly, then putting his eyes back on the road. "Still have that boyfriend, yeah?"

That . . . takes me off guard. "Yep," I say. "Still have him."

"That's what I thought," he says, faking a sigh.

I shake my head and watch a sly grin spread on his face. Is he messing with me? So I nudge him and smile and look back out the window.

Underground statues. Walls that make music. I wanted something different, new. I've been feeling stifled. Maybe this will remind me why I want to stay here. Maybe this will keep me more grounded. Maybe this is what I needed all along.

TWELVE

Chase pulls into a parking garage and drives up the ramp past a few empty spots. "You missed a few spots."

He grins. "I know."

He keeps driving up and up until we get to the open-air top level.

"What are we doing up here?" He parks and I get out of the car and straighten my shirt.

"Best view." I look up and he smirks, a half smile that doesn't quite reach his eyes. With a raise of his eyebrows, he gestures for me to look to the side. I turn and immediately understand.

The sky is huge around us, vast and endless. I've never seen the sky like this before—dark black, but feeling transparent, vast, with a banana-shaped moon in the center. I walk to the edge and hold on to the railing. It's cold and wet in my hands, and I look up at the stars. There's so much light from all the tall buildings, so you can't see many stars. But the skyline is impressive.

"Cool, right?" Chase whispers.

"Yeah," I say. "I've lived here my whole life and never seen this view."

"What's the view by you?"

"Not as bright. We don't have tall buildings, so when you look up it's all stars. They're all around you."

"That's cool, too."

"Yeah."

I look down the six stories and see people wandering around through the lit streets. They look so easy to move from here, like I could pick them up and put them at the place they're going to. If only it were that easy.

"Do you have an ID?" Chase asks.

I furrow my brow and say, "I don't drive yet." But as the words come out, I realize what he means. "Oh, no, I don't."

"It's okay. Let's go," he says and walks to the elevator.

"Where are we going?" I ask. "I want to tell Sam."

"I heard some people were at a club, so we'll go there first."

"The . . ." I start, but don't continue because I'd rather be surprised. So I just tell Sam that. It makes me want to text Faye and tell her what's going on, but I don't even know what to say. I haven't mentioned Chase much, and I don't know how to explain how I ended up here, with him, and not home doing nothing. What she assumed I'd be doing.

Maybe it's okay to not do what's assumed.

When we get out of the parking garage, we're in the middle of downtown Orlando. Horns loud, music blasting, crowded sidewalks. It's dark out, but the lights are bright. I'm energized.

"We gotta get food at some point; I'm getting hungry," Chase says and walks to the left. We pass a long line of people, all waiting and chatting outside. Everyone looks super laid-back, and I feel better about my simple blue thrift-store dress. At the front of the line is a guy taking tickets, and I look at the billboard to see what's going on. The Pepperpots are playing—I've heard of them.

"Know them?" Chase asks, noticing me look.

"Yeah, local band," I answer.

"Really? They seem pretty popular."

"Graduated a few years ago, I think; they've been touring," I say, seeing that he's right—they are popular. Someone from here is doing something big. It's possible. I never thought of that.

"That's the lead singer," I continue, I guess kind of proving that I know someone cool. Not that I know him, but I know who he is. I point to a guy looking at the line from around the corner. He's smoking, and I can tell from his stance that he's pleased with the turnout.

"Cool," he says.

We get to a club that's collecting IDs at the door. The outside is nondescript—just brick and a dark wooden door. No sign.

"I don't have—"

"I know," Chase assures me, putting his hand on my arm. "It's cool."

We walk forward and I kind of walk behind Chase a little, hoping to blend in so they don't see I'm without an ID. Maybe they'll let me in if it looks like I'm with him.

The bouncer—a larger guy with a shaved head and tight black shirt over some noticeable muscles—looks at us and says, "IDs?"

Chase takes out his, and says, "She forgot hers."

He pulls out a yellow band and puts it on Chase's wrist. Then marks my hand with a black *X*. "C'mon in," he says, waving us through.

"Well, that was easy," I say, and he puts his hand on my shoulder and steers me deeper into the club.

The walls are brick and the lights are low. There are weird dolls hanging from the ceiling, and the artwork reminds me of the Haunted Mansion. "Where are we again?" I ask.

"Back Bar," Chase says. "It's cheap and easy to get into if you're under eighteen."

"And there's dancing." A voice pops in, and we both turn around to see Kate. "Hey, Chase," she says, slinking her arms around him. He holds her close, and her dress goes up impressively high. When they let go, she's giggling, until she turns to me. "Penny."

"Hey," I say, matching her nonenthusiasm.

"Everyone's already dancing," she says, grabbing Chase's hands and pulling him behind her. Disappointment hits me hard as I realize this is the night I'm having. I'll probably just be dragged behind. I pull out my phone as I walk to see if Sam called, but find just one text.

> UGH can't tonight. No car. See you Monday! I'll want all the details. Have fun! ;)

Ugh. Indeed. It's good she's not here, but . . . now I get to deal with this on my own. And I have no way of ducking out. I take a deep breath in and ready myself for the night. Maybe it'll be fun after all . . . right?

I turn the corner and am surprised to find an entire dance floor on the other side. It's down a few steps, sunk into the club. Lights are bright, illuminating every surface in the room. Beams of pink and orange and blue are weaving around the dance floor. The music is loud, and there's a giant TV screen that's playing music videos on the back wall. Chase, alone, looks back at me.

"I think we lost Kate," I shout over the music, watching her fly back to the dancing, tossing a meet-me-here look back to Chase.

"That happens," Chase says, then points to an empty small booth. It's still early, so not a ton of people are here yet. Some are dancing, some mingling, but the booths are empty.

"Have you been here before?" I yell over the music.

"Yeah, last weekend."

"The weird-statue-and-musical-wall weekend."

"Yep. Not so much my scene."

"What is your scene?" I ask.

"I don't know. More casual? I'm gonna get a drink—want anything?"

"Nah, thanks." I've never really drank before; haven't had the opportunity. Logan and I had sips of champagne on New Year's Eve, and Faye snuck us some of her mom's wine once, but I didn't like either. As soon as he leaves, Kate pops back up.

"Hey," she says, sitting across from me.

"Hi," I say awkwardly, tucking my hands under my legs.

"So what's going on with you and Chase? Everyone wants to know."

"Who's everyone?" I shake my head and say, "We just rehearse together sometimes. Besides, I have a boyfriend."

"Boyfriend?" she asks skeptically, and I can't help but feel offended by her reaction. "Okay, good. 'Cause I know a few girls who are interested."

"Including yourself?" I ask before I can stop myself.

"Maybe," she says with a sly smile. "Where's your friend Samantha? I thought you guys were joined at the hip or something."

"We're not," I say, offended. "She's at home." I realize that sounds lame, so I add, "With a friend. She's hanging out with other friends."

Kate nods. "Sure she is."

Before I can ask her what her deal is, she wanders away, back to dancing. I'm incredibly irritated by the time Chase gets back, Kate's words still echoing in my head.

"What I miss?" Chase asks, standing by the table.

I'm about to tell him what Kate said about Sam, but decide against it. "Nothing," I say. "Though I think some of the girls from camp are happy you're here," I add.

"Hmmm," he says, looking at them. I watch as he takes a sip of his drink and question once again why he's here with me. And not there with them.

A song comes on that I don't recognize, and everyone starts cheering and singing along. And it feels like there's an inside joke going on, and I'm not part of it. I turn back to Chase and he's kind of moving his head to the beat slightly.

"Did you want to dance?" I ask.

"Not really," he shakes his head. "Still hungry, actually. Let's go next door." He finishes his drink in a gulp, tosses the cup into the trash, and stands up. It all happens so fast, I just find myself following behind him, trying to keep up. I wonder why we even came here in the first place, but then he goes over to Kate on the dance floor and says something into her ear. She pulls back and looks at him, then kisses him on the cheek.

I follow him next door to a loud and bright pizza shop. It's tiny; there are only four tables, and three are taken. I sit down at the fourth while he goes to get food. I'm not hungry.

"This place kind of sucks, but it's here," he says, sitting down across from me. He puts a piece of pizza in front of me.

"I wasn't hungry," I say.

He shrugs. "My dad says it's rude to eat alone."

"What do your parents do?"

"Dad's a lawyer, so he has *rules* about things. Like eating alone. It's probably because he's never eaten alone, ever," he says, shaking his head. I want to know more about that, but I don't feel like I should ask. He seems closed off; it's his tone.

"And your mom?"

He sighs and shakes his head. "It's embarrassing. She writes romance novels."

"That's not really embarrassing," I say.

"Not, like, sweet romance novels. Like, those cheesy ones where the guy is all buff and shirtless on the cover. And, like, a mysterious prince knocked up his secretary."

I start laughing. "No! That's amazing."

"And embarrassing."

"Your mom writes trashy novels!"

"I don't think the people at the other tables heard you," he says, looking around, but a smile is breaking through.

"Oh my god, my mom used to read them. She had a stack of books on the floor she used to get from the library.

Tons of these tiny red books with bare-chested doctors on the covers. I bet she read some of your mom's."

"She has these events, and I have to go sometimes. And they just all talk about hot guys and, ugh, it's just so gross. They're like *forty*- and *fifty*-year-old women. Talking about shirtless dudes."

I start laughing. "I was *not* expecting that from you."

"You're not making this any better," he says.

"I'm sorry, I'm sorry." I pause. "Do you get to pose for the covers?" I giggle.

"I think you should leave," he says, but he's laughing now, too.

"Is she writing one now?"

"Probably? I don't know. She's either hiding in her room writing, or on a writer's retreat, or promoting a book. She's, like, *always* missing."

"You don't go to all her events with her?"

"Just the local ones. She went to London for some romance writers festival last year. I joined her for that one—that was cool. Your turn. Please tell me your parents are, like, sex therapists or something, because that'll make this even better," he says.

"Not as interesting," I say. "My dad owns a small diner in Christmas—it's a family place, passed down from my grandparents."

"And your mom?"

I pause. "She died a few years ago."

"Oh," he says, eyes wide and looking concerned. "I'm really sorry."

"No, it's okay," I say, shaking my head. "It's been like five years. . . . I mean, it's *not* okay, but it's okay." He looks down, and I know the question he wants to ask, but isn't. So I answer for him. "Car accident, in our town. Drunk driver."

"Really?"

"Yeah . . ." I say, looking down and remembering the closed casket. "So, yeah . . ."

"Okay." He pauses.

"So . . . are you going to run the diner?"

"Hmmm?" I ask, still kind of in a daze.

"You said your dad's restaurant is passed down—are you getting it? Or, like, a brother or sister?"

"No brothers or sisters," I say, realizing what he's asking. Realizing that I inadvertently told him my future. "But, yeah, that's the plan. Eventually, I'll get it. After college and stuff."

"I mean, that's kind of cool. You know what you're going to do."

"Yeah," I say.

"But also that means you're stuck, right?"

"Not stuck. Just . . . planned, I guess."

"I guess having a plan is better than not having a plan."

"I guess. I'm not going to Hollywood or anything."

He leans back and crosses his arms. "I think you go for

something if you want it. If you don't want it enough, you don't try."

"So . . . are you saying I'm not trying in camp?"

He waves his hands. "No, that's not it." Pause. "Well, okay, maybe. I think you're great in camp, you know that, but I think you could be better if you wanted it more. Maybe you don't because what's the point? You're staying here."

I'm a little put off by this. "So you're saying if I want a huge career for myself in the future, I'll act better now?"

"No, I'm saying if you're not afraid to want something, you'll be better. You're not letting yourself be afraid."

I think that over for a second, then reply, "So you're a better actor because you want to go off to L.A., then?"

"No . . . I'm a better actor because I'm not afraid to want to act. I want it. Even if I didn't have this huge future plan, I'd still want to act. And I think you're afraid of that."

"You barely know me, Chase," I say. "How could you know that?"

"I am astonishingly observant." He grins in this annoying way. "Your audition was amazing because you really wanted it. Keep that fire."

"The college here has a theater program. I want to do it while in school. I just know that I won't go much further."

"Why not?"

"Not good enough?" I shrug. "That and, like I said, prior obligation."

"So let me ask you—why do you act?"

"Because I love it," I answer honestly. "I kind of fell into it. I wanted to try some after-school program while Logan—my boyfriend—was at baseball practice. So I tried it. And kind of never left the drama room."

"Why do you love it?" he asks.

"I don't know. . . ." I say. "I feel like me when I'm acting, even though I'm not, you know. I never really had something that felt like me—Logan had baseball his whole life and everything. And my mom had cooking. So acting seemed, I don't know, natural? Like I wasn't horrible at it—I was pretty good. I *am* good. I don't know what I'm saying," I partially laugh. "It just feels right."

"That makes sense," he says. "I feel the same. There's, like, no other option, right?"

"Yeah," I say. "What do your parents think?" I ask. "Of your acting and stuff?"

He shrugs. "Don't know. They've seen a few things, but are just baseline supportive. You know, they'll cheer for me and whatever, but not, like, care about auditions or anything."

"So they don't know you were cast as Tom?"

"Nah. I'll tell them when the show's premiering."

"My dad's pretty supportive. He's run lines with me and stuff."

"That's cool. My dad rehearses cases with me. But not really with me, more so just says facts out loud and I nod sometimes."

I think of my dad at home holding my script. Of him doing voices even though I tell him not to. I'm lucky to have that.

"Anyway," he says, finishing up his pizza in a few huge bites, "no more sappy talk."

"Oh, yeah," I say. "Did you, um, do you want to go back to Kate and them?"

"Sure," he says, standing up.

"Looks like they enjoyed your company." I grin.

"It is possible to flirt and not fall in love, you know," he says.

"But isn't that leading them on?" I ask, standing up as well.

"Sometimes people like to feel good. Let's go." He puts his arm around my shoulders and I stiffen. I still don't totally get him, but he just opened up a lot to me. And that means something.

Still, when he rubs my shoulder, I say, "I still have a boyfriend."

"And I still know," he says with a smile.

We get back into the bar, Kate and company are still dancing, one tangled mess. They've got a few guys around them, too, so they don't notice us at first.

"Dance?" Chase asks, and, you know, why not? I join him on the dance floor and start moving to the beat of the song. I close my eyes and let the feeling of the song take over. When I open them, Chase is looking at me with a smile.

"You're cute when you dance," he says loudly into my ear.

"Thanks," I say shyly, not used to other guys saying I'm cute. Logan was my first boyfriend. I've only had him.

Chase pulls me to him, and I put space between us because . . . I can't get that close. I can't, and I think he gets it because he gives me a knowing look and then pushes away.

At that moment, the girls come and descend on him. Kate's arms around his waist. And I fall to the back, not part of the action much anymore. I walk back to a table and check my phone. There's a message from Logan that I missed.

Hope you're celebrating!

I am, I think. *But not how we usually celebrate.* I go to answer, but don't know what to say. I can usually text him anything—*anything*—but right now I feel like whatever I type will be a lie. And I don't want that. So I click off my phone and look back to the dance floor.

Then there are hands over my eyes. I jerk back around and see a very happy, very smiley face.

"SAM!" I yell and jump up to hug her. "You came! I thought you couldn't!"

"I *couldn't*, but Jackson could."

She nudges a guy next to her and I recognize him from camp. I haven't met him yet. . . . He's super tall and skinny with dark skin and short hair.

I look back at Sam, and I think she gets what I'm mentally trying to ask her—*How do you know him?* "Our younger sisters are friends. We went to the same middle school and live by each other. Now we're in competing high school drama departments. Mine's better."

"Psshh," he says. "No way. We've got *legit* actors. You have—"

"The ability to stage *The Phantom of the Opera* next year!"

"Yeah, yeah, rub it in," he says with a smile. "Still bet my school would do it better if we could."

"Anyway," Sam says, turning back to me, "Jackson came to pick up his sister and I told him about you all partying tonight."

"And it was this or watching another Barbie movie, and let's be honest, I hate Barbie."

"I'm glad you guys made it." I smile and hug Sam again. "Chase is dancing with . . . um, some other girls from school."

"So let's go dance!" Sam says, dragging me onto the dance floor. When we get there, Jackson is out of earshot—instead saying hi to Chase—so I lean close and say, "Spill."

"Spill what?"

"You? Jackson? You've never mentioned him."

"He's just a friend!" she says, but she's blushing.

"Uh-huh. Just a friend. Well, let's make this night fun."

"What about you and Chase?"

I look over at him talking to Jackson and laughing at something. Kate is glaring. I look back at Sam and say,

"Still nothing between us."

"Well, let's make this night fun," she says, repeating me.

We dance for a while, mostly staying by ourselves, but occasionally with the guys. Jackson is goofy and fun, but with real talent.

"Trained in ballet." He winks at me and I shake my head in amazement.

After a while, I feel Chase's hand on my wrist. "Come on."

"What's up?" I ask.

"I have confirmation," he says with a smile.

"On?"

He doesn't answer, just winks and pulls me closer. "Let's go," he says.

"Wait, wait, Sam and Jackson. Not leaving without them."

He stares at me, then shrugs. "Go ahead."

I turn to Sam, who's now curiously looking at me. "Chase has some sort of surprise or something. Let's go check it out?"

"Sounds good!" she says, then drags Jackson off the dance floor.

"Where are we going?" I ask Chase once the four of us are outside.

"Surprise," he says.

"That's what they say in horror movies. I'm not about to be murdered," Jackson says.

Sam giggles and huddles close to me. We link arms and walk down the street like that.

There are people around us going in and out of bars and clubs and restaurants. A guy on the corner is holding a giant poster board that says we're all sinners going to hell, and not far from him, a few homeless people are sleeping on benches. We pass a church with giant stained glass windows, and girls walk by it in short skirts and high heels. We're not going in the direction of the car.

Finally, I stop Chase. "Come on, where are we going?"

"I want to show you something."

"What?"

"A wall that plays music," he says, and I get it. It's the wall he told me about. So I nod and follow.

"Nope, I want an explanation," Jackson says.

"You'll get one soon," I say, being just as mysterious as Chase.

Eventually, we get to the library. It's a large building, at least four stories. It's closed, but you can see the shelves through the windows. A giant clock tower is visible through the window closest to us.

"I used to go here as a kid. My parents took me to these magic shows," Sam says.

"They've got magic shows?" Jackson asks. "I'm in."

"Yeah." I nod. "Once at my library there was a live gator."

"Like, inside? Did it escape? What the hell?" he asks.

"No, no." I wave my hands. "It was part of a show. A gator

wrangler brought one for us to see. It was cool!"

"You and I have different definitions for the word 'cool,'" Chase says.

I smile. It's quiet where we are, much quieter than the main streets. We're off on the side, by businesses that are only open during the day. "Now show me this wall," I say.

We follow him to the side of the building, where a giant multicolored overhang covers four handprints on the wall.

"What is this?" Sam asks.

"Apparently a wall that makes music," I answer. We all stay like that, looking at the hands, but not moving. "I want to touch them," I say, walking over. I slowly outstretch my hand.

"Don't scare them," Chase says loudly as my fingers grace the handprint and I jump.

"Ugh," I say, frustrated as he laughs. Just for that, I push the hand. And . . . it makes music.

"Whoa," I say.

"Yeah," he responds. "Cool, right?"

It's a violin playing, a soft melody floating through the streets. Sam presses the next one and drum sounds pour out, giving a rhythm to the night. "This is so cool!" I say, pressing the next two buttons at the same time. "Sorry for doubting you."

"That'll show you," he says. I shake my head and continue pressing the buttons just to spite him. Sam does, too, and eventually the guys. We try to make a symphony, but mostly it just sounds like noise.

After a while, Chase stops and looks at me while the others continue to play. "I'd think you'd know about this. Since it's the library and all . . ."

"Huh?" I ask, then remember he picked me up at one. "Oh. Ha. Yeah. No." Which reminds me . . . where is he going to drop me off? I didn't think that through earlier. I told him to pick me up at the library because I didn't want him to see my home. But I can't exactly have him drop me off there, after it's closed. And I definitely can't walk home from there alone. And I don't want to ask Jackson, since I barely know him. So I'll have to . . . ugh.

We explore more of downtown, walking through the streets past tattoo parlors, smoke shops, and vintage clothing stores. We pass the vast lake, with its green fountain in the middle, sprinkling out water. Then we jump up on the rainbow-painted bandshell's stage.

I look out at the sea of chairs and breathe deep. Even in the dark it's wonderful.

Next to it is a sculpture of birds taking flight. We are those birds. We are flying through the night with nowhere to go, nowhere to be. We are free.

"Ready to head out?" Chase asks, and I nod. I hug Jackson and Sam good-bye, adding a "Call me later," whisper into Sam's ear. Then I follow Chase back to his car.

"Where to? Your house, or do you need to do some more reading at the library?"

"Funny. My house, but don't expect mansions or fancy

homes like in your town."

I direct Chase down the roads, under the overpass, and through the town I call home. It's night and there aren't many lights, but still—I'm seeing it through his eyes. The dinginess. The darkness.

He doesn't say anything, but I'm sure he's thinking it. He's putting it together as we pull in front of my small, one-story house. He parks on the street, not daring to go up the grassy driveway to the carport.

"Thank you. For tonight," I say, getting out as quickly as possible.

"Anytime," he says with ease, giving me a smile.

I stand there for a second, thinking of something else to say, but nothing comes. So instead I wave, and run up to my door, unlocking it and running in. When the door shuts behind me, I let out a breath I'd been holding in.

The night was so different from other ones I've had—so new and exciting. I'm used to being at Logan's house, or on Faye's street. I'm used to going to school and coming home. I'm used to the woods and the alligators and the normality of it all. It just makes me realize that if this is here, in somewhere I'm so used to, there must be so much more out there. Away from here.

I quietly walk to my room and notice my dad's light is off; he must have gone to bed. I walk back downstairs and notice his shoes are still gone. And his car . . . his car wasn't in the carport.

I wonder where he is.

I get ready for bed, and then finally answer the earlier text from Logan.

> Celebrated with some friends from camp. Wish you were there!
> Hope your night was excellent. xoxo

It's not a lie, not really. I did go out with people from camp. I just didn't specify that I mostly stuck with Chase, and that Chase picked me up and drove me home. I don't know if he'd be jealous, but . . . I don't want him to, just the same. Even though nothing happened.

But I don't want to think about that. Not now, at least. Not when the night is still whirling in my mind and making me wonder if it even actually happened. Making me think of the roof and the music and the sights and how there really is so much out there. I want to see it all.

THIRTEEN

When I wake up the next morning, Dad is standing in my doorway.

"WHA—" I jump, seeing him.

"Sorry! Sorry. I hate to ask this, but can you help out this morning?"

I look at the clock. "It's five a.m."

"I'll put on the coffee," he says, and that's that.

Ten minutes later we're in the car and I'm holding a mug. Despite knowing it's going to be hot out today, I wear long sleeves because early mornings make me cold. And tired. And ugh.

"How was your night?" Dad asks as he drives.

"Good," I croak out. "Went out with some camp friends."

"Oh yeah? Where'd you go?"

"Downtown," I say before realizing he'd probably not like that.

"*Downtown* downtown?" he asks, furrowing his brow. "I don't like you hanging out down there. It could be dangerous. There are fights in the clubs. Homeless people asking for money. Drinking."

"I didn't drink, Dad; don't worry."

"You didn't ask me if you could go."

"You weren't home." I sigh, not wanting to argue. But also seeing an opportunity. "Where were you last night, anyway?"

"Oh, out," he says, voice lighter.

"Out where?"

"Soccer match, remember?"

"Right. How was it?"

"Fine, we lost."

I want to ask him what time he got home, since he wasn't there when I did. And I wasn't exactly home early. But asking would mean admitting that, so maybe I won't go down that road.

"Who'd you go with?"

"Just a guy I know."

"You seem to have a lot of mysterious friends lately," I say jokingly, but he's not laughing. "What's up?"

"Nothing. We'll talk later."

"Umm, that's not cryptic or anything. Seriously, what's going on?"

He parks the car in front of the café and looks out the window solemnly before getting out of the car.

"Nothing. Nothing bad. Just not now."

"Dad . . ." I say, joining him out of the car. "Is it about your friend? Is it the café? Is something wrong?"

"Nothing. Everything is okay," he says, putting his hand on my shoulder. "Let's go work."

Dad unlocks the door and turns on the light. I've always liked the café early in the morning. It's peaceful—quiet, clean, undisturbed. In less than an hour, that won't be the case.

I methodically start wrapping silverware in dark red napkins and put them on the tables. I put out mason jar water glasses. I arrange the menus in a half circle. Everything is automatic—it's what I've always done.

I've been helping for as long as I can remember. At first it was just putting the silverware out. Then it was setting up. Then it was seating people. Then it was taking orders, serving food. Now? Now I know how to order dishes and food from the wholesalers. Now I know how to take complaints and accommodate. Now I know how to take over.

"Pen," Dad calls from the back.

"Yeah?"

"Waitress, section two."

"Got it." And that's what I'll be doing today.

An hour later and we're deep into breakfast and my face is hurting from smiling so much.

"Penny, we haven't seen you around all summer!" Ms. Summers, a regular for years, says when she sees me. She's around seventy, but I can't tell with all the makeup and the purple-gray hair.

"I've been in school!" I say, resorting to that. It's easier to explain than *I'm acting.* That requires me to talk about the role and the shows and the school and at least one person going, *Oh, aren't you fancy?* "School" sounds normal and requires zero questions.

"Always studying, that's our girl," she says. "Isn't she, Norm?"

"Yeah," her husband, a bald man who, when squinting at me, kind of looks like a turtle, says.

"I was just telling Norm, I was just saying how lovely you've grown up to be. Such a bright girl. Just like your momma."

I blush. "Thanks."

"And how's that boyfriend of yours?"

I smile. "He's great. He's working this summer."

"You two," she says, patting my hand. "Such good kids. Stay that way."

"We will," I say, not sure what that means. Does she think we'll suddenly derail?

"Now I'll have two eggs—you know how I like them, sunny side up, with bacon and a biscuit."

And that's how the morning goes. Person after person remembering my mom and telling me I'm doing great and telling me not to change and asking how Logan, my dad, everyone is. Everyone who's known me, every side of me, since I was born. Everyone who's seen me through all my stages. All expecting me here, doing the same thing.

By the tenth person I'm feeling claustrophobic, so I go outside, behind the building, to get some air for a few minutes.

"Pen?"

I turn back to see my dad peeking out from the red chipped-paint door. "Hey."

"You okay? You looked sick."

"Fine," I sigh. "I'm fine."

"What's wrong?" He looks back into the café, waves, and then walks outside, shutting the door.

"Nothing."

"If you don't want to work, that's fine. It's calmed down a little. We've got it; you can head home."

"It's not that. I love it here; I do. It's just . . ." I pause. "Have you ever felt . . . like . . . I don't know. Everyone here has known me since, like, diapers. And that's weird."

He nods. "Yeah, I'm familiar with the feeling."

"That's right, you grew up here, too."

He squats down next to me. "Never left."

"Did you ever think of going?"

"Honestly?" he asks, rubbing his chin. "Yes, repeatedly."

"Really?" I ask, surprised. "What made you stay?"

"Your mom, first. She had Country Time, and didn't want to leave it. So we stayed."

"So it's always been Country Time?"

"Well, and you. After she . . . I didn't want to move you. So we stayed. And that's good, right?"

"Yeah, I mean, of course. Our lives are here. But . . . but did you ever regret it? Staying here, and not seeing what else is out there. Did you ever regret it?"

He presses his lips together and looks away from me. He doesn't have to answer. That's answer enough.

I wonder what it would have been like, completely changing my life. Leaving everything I've known to start over. I shake my head—no, he did the right thing. I'm glad we stayed. I'm glad I had Logan and Faye and normality. After Mom . . . we needed normality.

But do I need that now?

"I have, yes," he finally answers. "But I'm glad we're here. What's best for you is what's best for me." I look down at my fingernails, not wanting to meet his eyes. "What're you thinking? You can tell me."

Dad stayed here for me. He didn't leave for me. He would have liked to; he sometimes regrets not leaving. This is all I know now.

I can't let him down.

"Nothing." I shake my head. "Thanks for staying for me. Now . . . let's go make some pancakes."

Monday marks our first day of rehearsals and I'm full of jitters. Sam's in the costume closet getting measured, so I find Chase and sit next to him on the edge of the stage. He has one knee propped up and is talking to the girl who got the role I'm understudying. She's shorter than me, with long black hair and a young-looking face.

"You'll be great," he says, then turns to me. "Oh, hey."

"Hey," I say, smiling, thinking about the night out, about how fun and confusing it was.

But he doesn't say anything else. He turns back around and they continue their conversation about her fears and doubts about the role, and he plays the gentleman who reassures her, such as he's done for me in the past. I'm just smart enough to not fall for him, and judging by her dreamy smile, I'm pretty sure she's not.

But still, I'm a little put off that he isn't talking to me right now.

I get up and walk backstage to the prop closet, where all the props are kept from every previous show. Not just for the camp, but for the college, too. There's a ton to pick from. I know they did *The Glass Menagerie* before, in 2001, so I'm hoping a lot of the stuff is left over.

I open the door and the smell of my grandparents' house hits me, nearly knocking me back. Mothballs and memories. I step inside.

It's more of a small room than a closet. Long and narrow. Boxes are stocked along the right wall, neatly labeled. The left side has some furniture pieces—small couches, coffee tables, lamps. It looks like a hoarder's room, actually, and very different compared to my school's prop closet, which is tiny and full of stuff either made or bought at the dollar store. The furniture pieces are usually borrowed. We keep everything as well, but nothing is really that fancy.

I was told I could use anything, and could even refinish or repaint if needed. I see a lamp that looks gold, and near it, a clock that looks like it might actually be from the 1920s. I pick it up.

"Hiding in here?"

I nearly drop the clock in shock, grabbing it just in time. I whirl around to see Chase leaning against the door.

"Helping out," I say, holding the clock up. "Teresa asked me to get some props. I do it for my school, too."

He squints his eyes. "What do you have to find?"

"I have a list," I say, pulling it out of my pocket. "I've marked off some bigger pieces already; they're not my responsibility. It's the smaller ones—like the clock—that I need."

He takes the list and looks it over quickly, handing it back without much of a reaction.

"I'm sure you can find most of that stuff here—I mean, I don't do behind-the-scenes work. But look at this place—it's like a treasure trove of props."

"You could say that." I nod. I turn back to my list.

"It's an illusion of truth. Everything here. It's all fake, but makes the room look real. An illusion of truth."

"Yeah," I say, staring at him. "Yeah, exactly." I'm about to comment on how perfect that phrase is, when I realize I already know it. "Act one, right?"

"You got me." He grins. "So is there anything you really have to find?"

"The collection of tiny glass figures my character owns. I know they did the play here, but I doubt they still have the glass menagerie."

He crosses his arms and says, "We should go find it, then. Tomorrow after rehearsal?"

I pause, smile, then say, "I thought you don't do behind-the-scenes stuff."

"I don't." He shakes his head. "But I always make exceptions for damsels in distress."

I put my hand on my hip. "I am *not* a damsel in distress."

He laughs. "That you're not. But those glass pieces? They are. And we need to find them."

"Deal," I say before I realize what I even agreed to.

After a few minutes, Teresa calls us all in to get started. The last two hours of camp each day are now reserved for rehearsal, so I look around and see who I'll be spending so much time with. I sit next to Sam and we highlight our lines in yellow and orange, promising to rehearse together later on. We do a basic read aloud for the script, and since I'm just an understudy, I don't say anything. I'm reminded, again, that I'll get one performance, and the girl in my role kind of scowls, and I wonder if it's because she won't be leading every night. And it's frustrating, just watching. Every time my character has a line, I ache to say the words, to make them mine.

I walk to the bus stop once we're through, wondering what the rest of practice will be like. Will I just be watching, or will I be participating?

I head right to Logan's. He's off today, and I know he's home with his brother. The night downtown pops into my mind and I don't know what to tell him. We tell each other everything, but I can't seem to bring myself to talk about my time with Chase. When I knock on the front door, to my surprise, his mom answers.

"Oh, hello, Penny! I was just talking about you."

"You were?" I ask, coming inside.

"I'm catering a wedding, and I needed someone to taste test." She looks over her shoulder and says loudly, "AND SOMEONE DOESN'T FEEL LIKE COOKIES."

"I *always* feel like cookies," I say.

"That's *exactly* what I was thinking." She smiles and walks back to the kitchen, and I'm left wondering how I became so predictable.

Logan comes out, and his hair has a bow in it. "Oh my,

what . . ." I can't help but laugh.

"Shut it," he says, taking the bow out. "Mikey decided I needed to wear Barbie's bow."

"I love that your mom got him a Barbie."

He shrugs. "He really wanted mermaid Barbie after watching *The Little Mermaid*. Except now the accessories end up in my hair." He walks over and hugs me, leaning his chin on my head. "How was rehearsal?"

"Meh—just okay," I say. "I'm still kind of disappointed with my lack of actual acting. I'm only an understudy, so I haven't been given much time."

"It'll get better."

"Penny, cookies!" his mom yells, and he disentangles himself from me.

"You're being beckoned."

We walk over to the kitchen and his mom has two plates set out.

"So, Penny, tell me about your camp. Logan hasn't said much!"

"Oh," I say, tasting a vanilla frosted one that looks like a heart. "It's good. We just started rehearsals today. I'm learning a lot," I say, using a pretty standard answer.

"How're the other actors?" she asks, whisking around the kitchen at the same time.

"Good, really nice. My friend Sam—Samantha—got a lead in our show, so I'm really happy for her. It's cool, she plans on going out to New York—to Broadway—after high school and, you know, try to make it."

"I'm sure her parents aren't too thrilled about that."

"Her moving away? I don't know. They'll probably miss her," I say, having never really asked that.

"'Probably' is right. And to a city like New York! I'm just glad you two aren't going anywhere."

"Yeah, yeah, yeah," Logan says, going to the refrigerator. I watch him open the door, get juice out, pour it into two cups, and put it back.

"Backyard?" he asks, and I nod.

"Thanks for the cookies!" I tell his mom, then follow him outside. Their backyard is small, and mostly taken up by a large tree with two swings hanging from it. We sit down and start to swing, the only noise comes from the squeaking chains.

"What's up?" I ask. "You seem off."

"Tired, I think," he says. "I've been with Mikey all day, so you know how exhausting that gets."

"I don't know how Faye does it every day." I shake my head.

"She must have so much patience. I love the kid, but . . ."

"Yeah," I say, scraping my feet against the floor. "You need a day off."

"Ha," he says. Then silence. "So, your friend Sam . . . She's moving to New York?"

"Yeah," I nod. "After she graduates. She's so sure of it—I mean, I bet if she doesn't get into a show, or get into college, she's still going to get up there. Like, it's meant to be for her. It's really cool, you know, how much she believes in her dream."

"Cool, yeah." He nods again. "What about your other friends?"

"From camp? Ummm," I start, because I haven't really told him much about the others. And come to think about it, I don't know much about them. "I'm only really friends with Sam. And Chase."

"Chase?"

"My acting partner? I've mentioned him," I say, hoping he remembers.

He nods his head. "Oh, yeah, sure."

"He wants to direct. In Hollywood or something."

"That seems so crazy, doesn't it?"

I tilt my head to him, letting the wind blow my bangs out of my face. "Directing?"

"Like, going across the country for a dream. That's not, you know, like, solid."

"Solid?"

"A sure thing. I mean, that sounds crazy to me."

"I guess . . ." I say, knowing what he's leading up to. There's an awkward silence.

"You're not . . . I mean . . . are you . . ."

I pause swinging, then start up again, trying to hide the pause. "No, of course not. I want to stay here."

"Okay," he says, visibly and verbally happier. "Okay. I

mean, you can if you want to. I don't want to, like, hold you back or anything, but . . ."

"But you don't want me to go."

"I want you to be happy."

"But you don't want me to go."

"I want to be with you."

"But you don't—"

"YES. I don't want you to go. Happy?" He grins.

"Very." I smile back, nudging him with my swing. "I don't want to go. I mean, I don't plan on going anywhere. I'm staying here. I *want* to."

"And not just for me?"

"Not *just* for you," I qualify, but even as I say the words, they're starting to feel rehearsed. Forced. Like I don't quite believe their meaning anymore.

"Good enough," he says. "I'm really happy you're enjoying camp and all, but I was just worried you'd want to, you know . . ."

"Try for more?"

"I guess." He kicks dirt, and it's strange, seeing him so insecure. On the field he's all ego and talk, but when it's just us, he's quiet and introspective. And sometimes, he's jealous.

"Hey, you have a whole new job, too. I don't know what goes on at those parties you go to."

"Oh, let me tell you. Last night was a man's retirement party."

"And he wanted a bounce house?"

"Yeah. Guess if it was a good idea."

"I'm going with no."

"Oh, not at all. I thought it was for kids there, or something, but it wasn't. It was actually for the retired dude. Everyone was in pain. We left early. Easy job."

I stop swinging and seriously eye him. "So you're saying some seventy-year-old ladies were totally hitting on you."

"You know how I am with seventy-year-olds." He grins. "Remember when we used to visit your grandmother at her retirement home?"

"Yes, all the ladies loved you. They kept asking you—not me—to come back."

"That's right."

I smile at the memory. "Do you have any parties tomorrow?"

"A birthday party during the day, I think. Not sure what else."

"Cool, well let's do something then. When I'm out of rehearsal," I say decidedly.

"Okay, what do you want to do?"

"You pick. Surprise me."

"Ugh, you know I'm not good at that. Remember the Chuck E. Cheese's fiasco?"

"I mean, you brought me there at the start of spring break and there were, like, seven thousand children."

"Okay, okay, I'll think of something better," he says,

grabbing my swing and pulling me to him.

I know it's not fair to compare Logan with Chase. And I'm not, really. But I just want that feeling that I had with Chase—of something new. And with Logan it's a hard feeling to have, considering we've known each other for so long. But I know it's still there. I know sometimes you have to work on things that are supposed to happen.

◇◇◇◇

Logan walks me home, and just as we get to the house, Dad is walking out the front door.

"Hey, Dad, going out again?"

"Hi, Mr. Nelson," Logan says, removing his hand from mine, always sure to be one step removed. I smile at his politeness.

"Logan," Dad says, nodding at him. "Yeah, and that doesn't mean you're having guests."

"Dad," I sigh.

"No, no, he's right, I'll leave," Logan says.

"You guys are ridiculous." I shake my head. "But seriously, where are you going?" *Again.*

Dad points to his shirt, and it's then that I realize it's the purple soccer jersey he always wears to games. I have a matching one, for when I join him. It's the one thing he treats himself to.

"That's right." I nod my head. "Sorry, forgot it was tonight."

"Playing against Toronto. It's been a tough season, but

I think we've got it," Dad says, then he explains the team's current place in the league to Logan, and I kind of zone out.

Logan's phone buzzes, and he furrows his brow. "Uh, it's work," he says, then steps away to take it.

Dad watches him, then looks at me. "I'm serious."

"I know, I know. You can trust me." He hugs me and he smells like syrup. "How was work?"

"The usual. How was rehearsal?"

"Fine," I say, again thinking of my lack of acting. "It was fine. I'm helping out with props on the show, like I do for school. I think tomorrow . . ." I start, then realize tomorrow is when I told Chase I'd go prop hunting with him . . . as well as when I told Logan I'd go out with him.

Oh shoot.

"Tomorrow?" Dad asks, raising his eyebrow, a habit I got from him.

"Nothing," I say, shaking my head. "Tomorrow I'll get a chance to act more. Since I didn't today."

"Good," he says. "Proud of you."

"You go enjoy your game," I say, and he smiles just as Logan walks back to us.

"Sorry," Logan says.

"Need a ride home?" Dad asks Logan, clearly a ploy for him to go.

"I, um, sure, Mr. Nelson." He looks at me, grabs and squeezes my hand, then walks over to Dad's car.

I watch as they drive away, wave, and feel a pit in my

stomach. I'm all alone. And I need to cancel one of my plans.

I head inside and as I look through the cabinets for dinner ideas, I see my phone light up.

"Miss me already?" I ask Logan, on the other end.

"Of course. So, the call I got? My boss. They need me tomorrow night after the birthday party."

"Oh," I say, feeling disappointed, but also relieved. "Okay, that's fine."

"I'm really, really sorry. Wednesday after work? Gives me more time to plan."

"Of course, that's fine."

"Really? Please don't be upset."

"I'm not upset! I completely understand. Love you."

"Okay, love you, too."

We hang up, and it's only then that I realize I didn't tell him about my other plans. I feel like I'm living two separate lives, and I have no idea when they're going to come together. Or if I even want them to.

FOURTEEN

Chase and I meet up after rehearsal and decide a local thrift store should have everything we need.

We walk into the small storefront in the strip mall twenty minutes from the college campus and start looking around. "I think we need this," I say, picking up an ornate portrait of a very old man scowling at us.

"I think *you* need it," Chase says, putting it back down. "Aren't we supposed to be looking for glass things?" We chose this place because it's a fancy thrift store. There's a ton of weird stuff, but also name-brand clothes and bags. Because of that, everything costs a bit more. Thankfully, I'm using the school's money.

"Also, don't we already have our dad's picture to use?"

he asks, referring to the portrait I have to find that'll represent our characters' father.

"Yeah, just thought this would be a fun addition."

"I don't look like him," he says seriously.

"I was just kidding," I clarify. He stares at me, and then cracks. "Jerk," I say.

"See, that's why I like you. You don't take my crap."

"That's why I *don't* like you. You give me crap." I walk away from the frames, to the more decorative area—plates, cups, statues, and the like.

"You lie," he says, leaning against the aisle with his arms crossed.

"Hey, look," I say, picking up a set of clear plastic Mickey Mouse figures.

"Glass?" he asks.

I shake my head. "No, feels like plastic. But people won't notice, right?"

"Nah, they'll be perfect. How many do you need? Is that enough?"

"No, I need a lot more. My character lives through these little pieces. They're her babies. She needs enough to feel like she's needed." I pause. "They're her big, beautiful world, but they're fake and fragile."

"She's so weird."

"No, just damaged," I say simply. "She has problems; she's a very quiet character. She stops going to school because it makes her too nervous. She never leaves the house. She stays and takes care of this glass collection. She has social anxiety, and only feels comfortable at home."

"Well, someone did their homework."

"If by 'homework' you mean studying my character and the script, then yes. How's learning your lines going?"

"Good." He shrugs. "It's not too hard. I mean, there are a lot, but I can get it done."

"And how's getting into character?"

"I *am* Tom."

I roll my eyes and walk to another aisle. "Are you?"

"Yeah, totally. Tom's stuck in a small town, wanting to escape. That's basically me right now. I'm drawing from personal experience."

"Small towns are not that bad," I say.

"I'm just saying this is a small town with small lives. I want something bigger."

"It's not that bad here, really."

"But you've never been out of here," he says. I start to answer that I have, but I haven't. Not really. "Speaking of, my parents are out of town this weekend, so party at my place."

"Really?" I ask.

"Of course." He waves me off. "Bring your boyfriend."

"Yeah, okay," I say, already knowing I probably won't. It won't be Logan's crowd. He won't fit in, and then he'll feel uncomfortable. That's how it went when I brought him to a cast party for my last couple of shows. He liked the people and talked to some of them, but he just stood off to the side for most of the time. And then I felt bad and left early. And then he felt bad for making me leave. And it was a mess.

But I also kind of like having this other side of me right now that no one else knows about. This other world I'm still learning about, still exploring. And I guess I want to keep that to myself, for only a little bit longer.

Chase follows me around the aisle and peeks over. "Okay, getting those? I've got another place we can check out."

We pay for the plastic pieces and head to another thrift store a few miles away. Then a flea market and another thrift store. We find thirty pieces in total, and it's more than enough. We have animals and people, sea creatures and fairies. We have a little bit of everything. And each time we find a new one, I find myself getting closer to the menagerie, piecing it together as if it's actually mine. In the last store, a used clothing store, we finally find a unicorn.

"It's perfect," I say, holding it up to the light. "I can't believe we found one."

"You know, a unicorn without a horn is just a horse. Even broken it could be something."

I look at him through the glass piece and smile. It's part of the script—not word for word, but part of it. Laura's favorite piece is the unicorn. It's unique and different, just like her. But then it's broken, and she has to learn what it's like being a horse.

"You're gonna be a great Tom."

"And you'll be an all right Laura."

"Gee, thanks," I deadpan. I cup the unicorn in my hand and keep walking around the store, thinking of the play, of Laura. Of her character's life and mine. Of the tiny pieces of glass breaking off the unicorn, and her turning it into something different, something new. Maybe that's what I have to do. Chip away at my days some more until they resemble something new and different and inspiring.

◇◇◇◇

I get a text from Sam, but wait to answer it until I get home. Rather than texting her back, I call.

"There you are!" she says.

"Here I am," I say, and smile. It's deadly hot out, but I don't want to be inside, so I sit on a chair outside our house, feet propped up on a low wall blocking our overgrown and unmaintained garden.

"Where'd you go after practice? I was going to see if you wanted to grab ice cream and chat or something. My friend from school found this bootleg download of the original *RENT* cast performing at the New York Theatre Workshop, like, pre-Broadway."

"That's so cool! How is it?"

"Gritty, in the best way. Like, it wasn't polished for

Broadway yet, so it had some songs that didn't make the cut. And they weren't perfect, but you totally got why they were added at the time. And nothing was, like, perfect and I loved it. The voices, god."

"Amazing."

"Seriously amazing. It's weird that people only know Idina Menzel for playing Elsa now."

"This is the second conversation in the last week that Elsa was mentioned," I laugh. "Logan was renting out a bounce house for a woman who was having Elsa at her daughter's birthday party."

"Like, the real Elsa?"

"Ummm," I say. "You know Elsa is fake, right?" I smile.

"You know what I mean. How's Logan?"

"Oh, he's good," I say, remembering that at this very moment we should have been on a date. "Working a lot."

"I'm still convinced he's imaginary," she says, a joke in her voice.

"I promise you he's not."

"Then why haven't I met him?!"

"You will, soon."

"Uh-huh."

"At Chase's party," I say, without thinking. "Er, Chase just told me he's having a party this weekend. So I'll probably bring Logan."

"Ohh, I haven't heard about this party yet. Oh man, yes, we have to go. It'll be so fun. Also, wait, is that where you were after school? With Chase?"

"Um . . ."

"You were."

"Not like that, jeez," I say.

"Details, please."

I smile. "We just went to buy some pieces for the menagerie."

"How was it? Did you find pieces? Did you fall in love?"

"Again, I have Logan. No, it was fine, fun. He was cool. That's it, nothing too exciting to report."

"Boring."

"Why don't *you* go for Chase?" I ask, almost wondering why I haven't asked her this yet.

"I don't know, he makes me nervous."

"He makes *you* nervous?"

"Yeah! I don't see myself, like, sitting down and having a heart to heart with him."

She's right, I can't see that, either, unlike Logan, who I can spill my guts to at any moment. He's reliable, in a way I guess I never quite saw. All the times he just sits and listens—he's present.

"Hey," she says, drawing my attention back. "I'm having trouble with a scene—want to rehearse again?"

I smile. "Yes, please. I liked the table read we did today, but it wasn't enough. I'm still number two, and it's so annoying."

"Well, tomorrow we're supposed to be in groups, so

hopefully that'll be better and you'll get more time onstage. Do you want to come over?"

"I don't have a ride right now," I say. When I got home from the thrift stores, there was a note from Dad saying he was out bowling. It's another night he's out, another night he's not talking to me. I texted him to say I was home, that I'd see him soon, but he just sent a quick "okay" back. I'm worried. "Let's just do it over the phone," I continue.

"Okay!" she agrees.

I go inside and get my script out of my bag. It's crumpled and worn, like all well-loved scripts are. I lie down on my bed and open it up. "First scene?"

"Oh yeah."

◇◇◇◇

The next day Logan and I have our perfect date.

Only it's not so perfect.

"This wasn't exactly what I had in mind when I said 'surprise me,'" I say, walking with Logan up to the World's Largest Fake Alligator.

"But you *are* surprised, right?"

"I mean. Yes. Sure," I say, and then I start laughing. Because I meant outside of Christmas, not right in our backyard. I'd been to the park before—it's a nature conservancy with alligators and tigers and stuff. My dad took me when I was younger so I could feed the animals. It was pretty cool back then, but not really something I'd want to revisit. Especially considering I don't think it's been updated since

I was a kid, judging by the World's Largest Fake Alligator's chipped and faded paint job.

"We don't have to go if you don't want to," he says.

"No. We're here. We should go. It'll be fun," I say. "I guess . . . let's get swallowed?" I ask, nodding toward the entrance, which is, in fact, through the World's Largest Fake Alligator's mouth. The entire ticket counter AND gift shop are inside as well.

"Wait, wait, we need to document this," I say, getting out my phone. I have Logan pose on top of one of the teeth and I snap a photo. Then we take a picture of the two of us looking scared as we're going into the belly of the gator.

"This is the most ridiculous place in the world," he says, then feels his pocket. He pulls out his phone and furrows his forehead. "Mom," he says, then answers.

I walk away so he can talk, and take in the detail of the inside of the alligator. Mostly, it's just slick and kind of off-white. I'm sure at one point this was the coolest theme park, but then the rest of Orlando came to be, and this fell by the wayside. My dad calls this Old Florida.

A jingle plays in the background, an old-timey banjo number, and for some reason the downtown Orlando library's musical wall comes to mind. That was something different, something unique to see. The old fake alligator . . .

"Y'all ready for a treat?" a voice asks, and I turn around to see a guy who works here. He's in khaki shorts and a matching khaki shirt and hat. He has his hands on his waist and waits for us to answer. I look at Logan, who's still on the phone, and say, "Yeah, soon," with a smile, nodding to Logan.

The guy nods, then walks back behind the ticket counter. Guess it's pretty dead this time of day.

"Crap," Logan says with a sigh.

"What's going on?"

"Gotta go home. Mom's been called for a last-minute job and can't bring Mikey. It's a baby shower, so no kids—germs or something like that."

"Oh," I say, trying to not let my disappointment show. "Okay, that's fine."

"It sucks. I'm sorry. Another night?"

"Of course," I say, holding his hands. "Maybe somewhere with less fake gator?"

"If you insist," he says with an exaggerated sigh. I squeeze his hands and follow him out.

"Hey, there's a party coming up."

"Yeah?" he asks.

"At my friend Chase's house this weekend. His parents are out of town."

"Oh," he says. "Cool. Are you going?"

We get to the car, and immediately he turns on the AC to cut through the heat. "Yeah, I'd like to. Sounds like fun, right?"

"Uh, sure."

"I mean, you can come, too, of course!" I mention,

wondering what he'll say, how he'll react. Maybe this could be a different type of date for us.

"When is it?"

"Saturday," I say as he turns on the ignition, paying more attention to the car than to me.

He sighs. "Working."

"Oh," I say, half disappointed and half relieved. I shouldn't feel that way.

"Yeah," he says. He's quiet for the rest of the drive back to his house.

Logan's mom is in full-on panic mode when we get there. "I'm so sorry I had to cancel your date," she says, running from room to room. "Order pizza, my treat."

"It's fine, Mom. Go," Logan says, holding the door open for her.

"This is my first baby shower, you know," she says, grabbing her keys. "Have to go to the shop and start baking. Baby stuff is so much more fun to make than wedding cookies. So much cuter! I remember when you and your brother were cute," she jokes to Logan.

"Ha-ha," he says.

"You'll have cute kids at least," she says, picking up her bag.

"*Mom*," Logan says, grabbing one of the trays and helping her out. The door shuts and I'm left in the living room, kind of standing there in a panic. *Kids?*

A parade of footsteps breaks my thoughts and I see

Mikey running to me. "Are you hanging out tonight, too? Cool. You can be Catwoman when we play Batman. I'm gonna be Batman because I'm the man!"

I turn to him and break out of my thoughts. I can't think of that now. I don't want to. I laugh and answer, "Yes, you are. And of course I'll be Catwoman."

"You the bad guy. You can steal all the jewels from this," he says, giving me an empty shoe box.

Logan comes in and raises his eyes at the shoe box. "My loot," I say. "Since I'm Catwoman and all."

"Ah," he says. "And that makes me . . ."

"Joker. HA-HA-HA-HA-HA."

"All right, then," Logan says, and scoops his brother up, throwing him over his shoulder. We play like that until dinner, and even then we play some more, pretending each chicken nugget is a different character to get Mikey to eat something other than French fries. Once he goes to bed—after much resistance—I collapse with Logan onto his bed. I should go home, but I don't want to yet.

"Thanks for staying with me," he says, rolling on top of me.

"Of course," I say. "Mikey is wonderful."

"Wonderfully active," Logan answers. He kisses me gently. And while I kiss back, I don't feel completely . . . into it. Maybe I'm just tired. His hands go to my waist and when I feel them on my skin, I push them away.

"Hey, you okay?" he asks, breathing deeply.

"I . . . don't know," I say honestly.

"Are you upset about tonight? I know it sucks that we couldn't go out. . . ."

"No, it's not that . . . I just . . . I don't know."

"Pen . . ."

"I'm just—I don't want to think about babies." I say, probably too loudly. Then I backtrack. "Sorry, sorry, that was crazy. I mean, maybe one day, sure, but not now. I'm seventeen."

"Okay . . ." he says slowly, letting go of me. "I don't want to have babies right now, either. At all. Why're you bringing it up?"

"Your mom," I sigh, flipping my hand up.

"Oh god, don't listen to her. You know she wants us to get married as soon as possible and then have, like, a million children right away."

"And what do you want?" I ask, because I'm not sure if it's that different.

"I want you," he says, pulling me to him again.

I fall into his kiss. It's easy for Logan—he's so sure of everything. But reservations are coursing through me, and it's getting harder to ignore them.

FIFTEEN

As rehearsals become more frequent, it's easy to forget my fears and lose myself in the role. I typically sit with the other three understudies and we practice together while the leads are doing their thing. We take in the notes given to the leads and copy some movements/deliveries, but also try to bring our own motivations to the roles. It's hard, though, because we get little feedback, since all of the attention is put on the leads.

I watch Sam on the other side of the stage. She's perfecting the role, but I can't help but feel jealous. She's with the *real* cast and I'm not.

And when I'm not rehearsing, I sit in the back and organize the props. I set new coats of paint on frames; I make sure all the plates match. I don't need to go out shopping much more, but I do need to keep everything in order.

Teresa calls us all together, and the eight of us sit in a line on the stage. "Okay, today we're going to mix it up a bit. We need our understudies to rehearse, too, for their night, and in case of anything," she says. "I want everyone as knowledgeable about this show as possible. I think what's best would be to rehearse today with someone else. We'll have two separate casts going at the same time, each half regular, half understudy. We'll rotate out again tomorrow. I want us to be able to act with one another flawlessly."

There's some rumbling from the leads, and I wonder if they'll object.

As if on cue, the girl playing my role says, "Um, I don't think it's smart to do that right now, when we're still getting show ready. Why mess it up?"

"No, this is necessary. As an actor, you have to be ready for new challenges, and this may be one. You have to think about all actors, and not just yourself. Okay, I'll go by who's sitting together for today—presumably this will make the switch easier. Jackson and Chase, you're with Penny and Sam. Which leaves the rest of you together."

Sam gives me a high five and we meet up with Chase and Jackson on the right side of the stage.

"I feel like I'm mingling with royalty," Jackson, the understudy for the other male role, says, crossing his arms and smiling. Since we hung out with him downtown, he's been super fun to work with. We've perfected the us-versus-them mentality. Sometimes, just to make me laugh, he'll do his scene with an accent.

"I'm so excited!" Sam says, and I smile. "Where should we start?"

"The beginning?" Chase asks, as if it's the most obvious thing in the world.

"Sounds good," Sam says.

We sit in a circle on the side of the stage, scripts in hand. By this point we're pretty familiar with our lines—especially those in the cast.

"Let's do it once like this, then again using blocking," Chase comments.

We all nod.

I feel the smooth wooden stage below me, and look out at the empty audience. And despite it being so private, I realize I'm nervous.

Chase starts his lines, and then Sam comes in. Jackson lies down on the stage, spreading his arms out, because his character doesn't enter until the last act. I'm thinking about that—our scene together—when I realize Sam's nudging my foot.

First line, and I already missed my cue.

"I'll bring in the blancmange," I say quickly. I just speak it, get it out quickly; I don't act it. I don't try to be Laura. A few lines in, I realize I'm doing just that—saying them, not really acting or feeling them. I'm usually so on when I'm with just Sam, or with the other understudies. It feels like that first day again, and I don't know what I'm doing. What's different?

"Penny?" Sam says. I look up and realize I must have drifted off.

"Sorry," I say, shaking my head. "Can we try again?"

Chase picks back up where we must have left off, start of scene two, and this time I'm trying a bit harder. The thing is, I know the script—I know it really well. I've read it what feels like hundreds of times. But I'm not getting that across. It all feels scarier all of a sudden.

I look up and see Chase and Sam looking at me. Even Jackson pops his head up. My cheeks go bright red as I look down in embarrassment. I can't believe I stopped listening. Again. "Okay, so, here's what I'm thinking. We get out of here," Chase suggests.

"What? We can't just leave rehearsal," I say.

"I'm not saying leave rehearsal. Let's just go backstage. Fewer distractions."

I nod my head in agreement, and we walk through the red velvet curtain, then over the curtain pulleys. Backstage is pretty much a giant wooden area with beams and costumes, pulleys and chairs.

"Dude, it's hard to act when all eight of us are onstage doing different scenes. Like, no privacy at all," Jackson says, I think mostly to calm me down.

"Let's use the prop closet," I suggest. "It's spacious and pretty private. . . ."

We walk in and all take different chairs or couches. It's quieter here, more secluded, and I'm somehow more nervous, if that was even possible. But then I think of Laura, my character, and how nervous she'd be. How weird it would be for her to be in a room with a guy by herself. And I know that feeling—I am that feeling right now. So I channel that. And I start acting. For real.

◇◇◇◇

An hour later, I shake off the character I had just been. It was amazing, actually feeling like I was someone else. Face blushing when she would, heart racing when hers did. I was more alive than ever, truly feeling like Laura, knowing I understood her more from my brief time with Chase, Sam, and Jackson.

"We rocked it," Sam says.

"We were awesome," I agree.

"How you handled the glass breaking? How you didn't cry but accepted it? Perfect," Sam says, and I blush.

"And how you yelled at Chase? I mean, I was scared of you!" I say.

Jackson jumps in. "And how I was clearly the best part...."

"You were fiiiine," Sam says, and Jackson jumps on her couch to poke her. "Stop, stop, stop! You were great!" She laughs.

I smile and look at Chase. He's looking quizzically at me.

"What?" I ask.

He shrugs and I shake my head at him.

"So what's going on tonight?" Chase asks.

"Home," Jackson says, stretching his arms over his head. "Promised my brother I'd play D&D with him."

We all turn to him.

"What? I'm a proud dungeon master. Don't you look at me like that."

"You are such a dork," Sam says, and I can't help but think she might be flirting.

"Says you," he replies.

"I'm going home, too," Sam says. "Babysitting my sister. Mom's going to this fund-raiser for work where she eats in the dark."

"Huh?" I ask.

"I don't know." She shakes her head. "She started to explain it to me, but I got confused. Why would you want to eat in the dark?"

"Oh, I've done that," Chase says.

This time we all turn to him.

"You said a fund-raiser, yeah? We had it in Atlanta. Basically, you eat in the dark to learn what it's like to be blind. I think some places do it to have you appreciate the food or something, but when we did it, it was that."

"Cool, but weird," Jackson says.

"Yeah, but my teacher had us go so we could become better actors. Like, learn to use different senses and stuff."

"That's cool," I say. "So since one sense is gone, you use the others more, right?"

"Right," Chase says. "You put a lot more thought into everything."

"I guess I should think of acting like that—not easy, needing thought."

"Yeah, exactly, something you shouldn't take for granted," Chase said. "Like, think about Laura. When she's with her glass, she's shy, but what does she hear? Smell? Think?"

"Hmmm..." I ponder.

"Exactly."

For some reason, I get really excited by this thought, by what I could bring to Laura, that I start making a mental note.

"I get it," Sam says. "I mean, feeling a character in all degrees... that makes sense. It helps you embody them more."

"But," Jackson cuts in, "wouldn't all this make you over-think the character?"

"That's a good point," Sam says, and I kind of agree.

"Shouldn't you? Get into character—shouldn't you overthink it?" Chase challenges.

"Maybe in the beginning, but not while onstage. That'll make it so unnatural. Like, just think about how annoying that would be, thinking about everything and not feeling," Jackson says.

I listen and I take it all in. Here I am, in a prop closet, having a debate over acting techniques. If only Logan and Faye could see me now.

◇◇◇◇

After rehearsal, we walk outside together.

"That was really fun," I say.

"Yes! Let's rehearse together some more!" Sam adds, and we all agree. She turns to me. "I'm so happy we got to act together today—*finally*!"

"I know!" I smile. I think of her acting—and how good she is in the role—and know I'm jealous, I'm completely jealous, but I'm also happy for her. So I give her a hug and laugh when she says, "Best cast ever."

"Need a ride home? I'm going that way."

"YES! Definitely," Sam says. I give her and Jackson a hug good-bye, then turn to Chase.

I'm about to say I've got a ride—the bus—but Chase says, "I can take you home, if you need."

"Really?" I ask, surprised. "It's out of your way."

"No worries, nowhere to go tonight," he says and I think of what he confided in me the other night. About his mom on tour. His dad always busy. Maybe he just wants company. Maybe that's what I am, someone to listen.

"Okay, thanks."

As we get onto the highway, I ask, "So if you weren't driving me home, what would you be doing tonight?"

"Honestly? Probably watching TV. New season of *Game of Thrones*."

"Haven't seen it," I say.

"What? Okay, we're going to remedy that one day."

"What's so great about it? Everyone seems to love it."

"Battles. Dragons. Hot girls. I mean, it has everything."

"Ah, so that's what you like in your shows," I laugh.

"Obviously." And he smiles.

"So maybe that's what Broadway is missing, to make it more appealing to people who normally don't like plays. Or think they don't."

"Like people who normally don't like dragon shows. Or think they don't."

"Exactly," I agree. "Is that something you'd like to work on? In the future?"

"I don't know. I want to do everything, you know? Not commit myself to a genre or role. I want to act and direct, I want to do action and comedy . . ."

I think about it, and ask him the one thing I've been wondering. "Aren't you scared?"

"To try? Not at all. What's the alternative? Staying at home with my parents?" I get what he's saying, because I know his situation, but at the same time I can't help but think about that for me. That's exactly what I'll be doing. And there's nothing wrong with it, but there's also nothing more there. "Look, I know I'm not going to get every role in the world. I know I won't be, like, a huge star the minute I start acting. But I *know* I'm going to do something. And in this field, you have to know or else you'll go nowhere."

"But what if you don't know?"

He shrugs. "Then you just figure it out."

I look at him and watch as the traffic lights from outside illuminate his profile on and off, on and off. Out of nowhere, a song pops in my head, one from the musical *Fun Home*.

Days and days and days. That's how it happens. I don't say it aloud, I just think it. In the musical she's showing how things happen slowly, days and days go by. How sometimes you just have to keep going because you're used to it, day after day. And that's kind of how I feel. I keep going, day after day, because that's what I'm used to. It's comfortable. It's routine.

"Still have the boyfriend?" Chase asks as he pulls onto my street.

"You know it," I say, like I always do. Thinking of all the days Logan and I have had together, and all the days we have lined up in the future.

He shakes his head and smiles. I do, too.

After Chase drops me off, I message Faye.

If you could do one thing tomorrow, what would it be?

Sleep. You're asking weird questions lately.

I'm serious! If you could do something different for one day, what would you do?

Hmmm, she responds, and the three dots meaning she's typing stay on the screen for a while. Travel. Out of the country.

I like that.

You?

Same. See what other cities are like.

Different places, same stuff.

How do you know?

I've got the internet.

I shake my head at her indifference.

Then why do you want to travel?

FOOD. Why the question?

I want to do something different.

Then do it. Don't wait for it to happen to you.

As I lie on my bed, I see a text come in from Sam.

So Chase drove you home.

I shake my head and respond:

And Jackson drove youuuuuu home.

Yeah ;)

WHAT IS THAT SUPPOSED TO MEAN?

NOTHING. He's cute, isn't he? I mean, really cute?

I smile and type back, **Very.**

I think of Faye and Sam and how they're so different, and yet similar in some ways. They've both opened up my tiny life to so much more. And I love them for it—each and every weird moment together. And today was no different. Today felt, I don't know, full. Like I lived a million lives all in one day.

A knock at my door interrupts my thoughts.

"Come in, Dad," I say.

"Hey, how was rehearsal?"

"Awesome," I say.

"Great. So happy for you," he says, looking down and shuffling his feet.

"What's up?"

"I'm going out again tonight, but I'll be home early, okay?"

"Oh my god, again, Dad?" I ask. "It's been, like, every night. WHERE are you going?" I finally ask.

He opens his mouth, then seems to settle on what he's going to say. "I'm going . . . I've been going on a few dates."

My heart stops just hearing him say it aloud.

"Oh . . ." I say, looking down at my hands.

Quickly, he adds, "I've been worried about telling you. I didn't know how. I tried a few times, but . . . I never knew how you'd react."

I don't know what to say. My heart is thundering in my chest. This is so new, so different. But not bad. No, I guess not. "I kind of . . . expected it. I mean, you've been secretive and stuff. But honestly, if you want to date someone, it's okay. It's been . . . five years since Mom . . ."

He lets out a breath. "You have no idea how relieved I am. That you're not mad." He finally walks fully into the room and kisses the top of my head. "Thank you."

I smile.

"You'll meet soon, I'm just . . . I'm just figuring things out right now."

"Uh-huh, of course," I say, almost in a daze.

"Unless you don't want to meet?"

"No!" I say. "No, I do. I'm just . . . still processing! Should I give you a curfew? Tell you no girls in your room?" I joke.

He smiles and gives me a hug. "Best daughter."

"Best dad."

"I'll call you when I'm coming home," he says, and then walks out.

I nod and lie back down on my bed. Dad is dating someone. Dad has a new life he's moving on to. Dad is discovering something new. He's making a new set of days. I wonder where they'll lead him. And me.

SIXTEEN

The next weekend I meet Faye at the library. "It feels like I haven't seen you in a million years," I say, sitting down across from Faye at a wooden table at the back of the library.

"Aww, you miss me." She grins, leaning back in her chair.

"You know it. But seriously, we've both been so busy—"

"*You've* been busy, from what I hear," she says, wiggling her eyebrows.

"What do you mean?"

"I saw Logan yesterday—he said you've been going out with camp friends a lot."

I fidget in my chair. "You were talking about me? Where'd you see him?"

"I was getting some groceries for my mom. He was doing the same."

"Oh," I say, then, "Yeah, I mean, kind of. We've all gone out a few times."

"I think he's jealous," she says, resting her chin on her hand.

"What makes you say that?"

She shrugs her shoulders. "I don't know, just how he said it. How he was kind of edgy about it."

"I'm not doing anything. I'm just hanging out with people."

"I know that, and I'm sure he knows that, too, but you know Logan."

"Yeah . . . ?" I ask, cocking my head to the side.

"He's . . . he's . . ." she starts, waving her hands, as if hoping the words will come. "Insecure."

"No, not Logan." I shake my head.

"Are you kidding? You so know he is. You've *mentioned* it before."

"Yeah, about baseball and his grades, but not about me. He knows we're . . ."

"The Perfect Couple," she says, emphasizing it. "I know, I know. You don't have to remind me. You may have to remind him, though."

I sit back in my chair and look away from Faye, at the books. We're in the designated teen corner—there are manga books stacked high across from me, and titles keep catching my eye that don't really help. *Love Hina. Love at Fourteen. Love*Com*. Why did we sit here again?

"This. This is why I don't do love," Faye says.

"You don't do love because you're stubborn." I smile.

"That, too. I'm waiting for college. Guys are more mature there."

"You sure about that?"

"They'd better be."

Beside the manga is a bookshelf with some board games, book displays, and crafts. There are coloring sheets that say "Everything Is Awesome." I get up and grab them, along with some crayons, from the display.

"What are we doing?" Faye asks.

"I don't know. I want to be creative."

"Is that why we're here? I haven't been to the library since I was, what, ten?"

"I came the other night. It's, I don't know, nice? Inspiring?"

"We're teens at a library on a Saturday. We have no life."

"We're totally cool," I say, picking up a blue crayon.

She rolls her eyes. "Whatever you say." She picks up a purple crayon and starts coloring. "What're you doing tonight? Big night with Logan?"

"No, he's working. And . . ."

"What?"

"God, this, like, proves what you said earlier, doesn't it? I'm going to a party at a friend's house."

"Oh man, what did Logan say to that?"

"That he's working. I mean, I invited him, but . . ."

She picks up another crayon. "He didn't want to go?"

"He already had his schedule. Do *you* want to come?"

"Ha, no. I'm good."

"I knew you'd say that." I smile. "Can I be honest with you?"

"Yes, always." She puts down her crayon.

I sigh and push my hair back. "I haven't introduced Logan to my theater friends yet."

"So? You haven't introduced me, either."

"That's because I know you'll hate them all." I grin and she shakes her head. "I'm kidding. It's different. You're my best friend; I know you're not jealous."

"Who says I'm not?"

I feel a jolt. "Are you?"

"No, of course not. I'm happy for you. BUT I can see your point. Logan probably is."

"Yeah, and I don't want him to feel that way, but I don't know how he'll be around my new friends. Not that they won't like him—obviously they will; he's Logan—but, like, he may be uncomfortable. They're all big dreamers and stuff, and he's . . ."

She finishes for me. "Logan."

"Yeah. You get it," I say. "I don't want to make him unhappy. I'm not *doing* anything, obviously. I love him. But I don't want to hurt him. I don't know how to feel about this. I want to go out, but I don't want to let Logan down. I want to keep doing fun things, but I don't want to lose Logan. This shouldn't be so hard. There shouldn't be an either/or for me having fun."

"Just be honest with him."

I pause, then go back to coloring. "I'm being annoying. How're you? How's the job going?"

She pauses, then picks up the crayon and starts coloring. "Good. Fine."

"That's descriptive," I joke.

"Not much to say. Kids are good. Two out of three are sick, but, you know, kids."

"Hours getting longer since it's the summer?"

"Extremely, which means more money. I'm at other houses more than my own. Which isn't bad, you know."

I pause and carefully ask, "How's your dad?"

She sighs. "Still unemployed and still blaming me, but that's how it goes."

"I'm sorry," I say, putting a hand on her outstretched arm. She shrugs as if there's nothing that can be done.

"How's the new kid?"

"New kid?" she asks, then a look of recognition hits her. "Oh, her, yeah, she's good. Yeah."

"I don't think you said 'yeah' enough," I joke.

"It's just . . . It's nothing."

"What's nothing?" I ask, looking over at her.

She pulls out her phone and looks at it. "Shoot, it's two, isn't it? I have to go."

"Huh?" I ask.

"Sorry, just saw the time. I really have to go. I'm late. Let's talk more later, okay?" she says apologetically. And I don't know if I believe her. Is she not telling me something? "Okay?"

"Yeah, okay. Talk later," I say. She comes over and hugs me. "Okay, now I know something's definitely wrong. You're hugging me. You don't do hugs."

She shrugs. "Some things change," she says with a slight smile, then walks out of the library, and I'm left watching her go and wondering what just happened.

◇◇◇◇

I leave the library and go over to the café.

When I walk in, I'm greeted by the typical bustle of a Saturday afternoon. I head to the back room and Dad is sitting at the desk, typing on his computer.

"Hey, Dad!" I say.

"Hey." He lowers the laptop and looks over at me. "How was the library?"

"Fine," I say.

"How's Faye doing?"

"Good . . ." I say tentatively. I still don't know what's going on with her.

He must have heard the hesitance in my voice, because he asks, "What's that mean?"

"I don't know," I say, flopping into a chair. "She was being weird. But it's Faye, so . . ."

"Uh-huh," he says. A coworker pops her head in to

update him on a few kitchen things.

"What're you thinking?" he asks. "You look like you're in pain."

I correct my face, surprised it looked like that. "Just thinking about the café."

He leans back, hands behind his head. "So, you surveying this place? Taking it from me already?"

"No! God, Dad."

"I was kidding. I'm holding on for as long as possible so you don't have to."

I tilt my head. "What's that mean?"

"Pen, whenever you talk about the future, you mention this place. You've forgotten things like . . . you know, college. Life."

"Well, yeah, but I also know what's in store later on."

"You say that like it's a bad thing."

"No! Of course not. This is Mom's. It means a lot to me."

He twirls in his chair and looks around. "It does, doesn't it? God, I remember her sitting back here, and me visiting her just like you are right now."

"Me too." I smile. "I used to draw in this seat." He twirls back to the desk and opens a drawer. He holds a notebook out for me. "Is this . . ." I gasp, taking it and opening it up to find my five-year-old drawings. Monsters and stick people. Puppies and horses. "Mom kept them?"

"Don't be so surprised," he says. "She kept everything."

"But this . . ." I grin.

He smiles, look down, then back at me. "I want to talk to you about something."

"About Mom?" I ask, still flipping through the pages.

"No, about you. And me." I look at him expectantly. He opens his mouth and then, as if refusing, closes it and shakes his head. "I don't want you worrying so much about everything. I want you to be seventeen and have fun. *Not too much fun*, but you know. I want you to do what you want, and not think about what I want."

"But wasn't that what I was supposed to be doing?" I ask, confused. "Mom told me from the start that my future was here, with the diner."

"If you want that to be true, then yes, I want that," he says slowly, as if carefully choosing his words. "You asked me the other day if I ever wanted to leave, and yeah, I did. There was a moment I didn't want to take over the diner. I wanted to continue teaching. But I knew I had to. For myself and for you. But you don't have that struggle—you just have you. I want you to do what *you* want."

I shake my head. "I want to be here with you."

"If you want that, great, but if you don't . . . I don't want you to hide who you are. And what you want. I love it here now, I love that I have you, but if I could have done some things differently . . . if I could have left . . . maybe I would have."

I shake my head. "Wait, do you mean the restaurant? Or Mom?"

"No! Not Mom. Never your mom. I mean after her."

"So you don't regret her?"

"Never. And I don't regret being here. I just want you to think about what you want, and not what I want. Consider your options. That's all," he says, then looks down.

"Okay." I nod. "I will." Maybe our conversation the other day sparked him to admit this to me.

And it makes me wonder—which, for me, is the life I'm meant to live? Am I going to regret doing what I had planned? Or am I going to regret not doing it?

◇◇◇◇

In my room, I lie on my bed, fiddling with my phone. It's Chase's party tonight. I want to go, but I have no way of getting there.

As if on cue, my phone buzzes with a text from Sam.

Going to Chase's?

I mentioned earlier about wanting to go, but I don't know now. I don't know if I'm in the mood to be happy and excited, when I'd much rather put on pajamas and eat a lot of ice cream.

I don't know. You?

YES! But only if you come.

I don't know! Not sure I'm in the mood. I don't have a car.

Stop. You are in the mood. And I'll pick you up!

Text address, be there ASAP.

Well, I guess I'm going.

I text Logan to remind him of the party, knowing he can't come but feeling like I need to tell him. Then I look through my closet for an outfit. It feels like the first day of school again, and I want to pick something that's not too overeager but not too low-key. I think of Chase and what his party might be like—obviously nothing like the sit-around-the-fire-pit parties I've been to before.

This will be fun, I tell myself. *This will be new and exciting.* Maybe that's what I need to get out of this feeling. Maybe I'll figure some things out with my friends.

SEVENTEEN

"Is this really his house? It's huge!" Sam says as we pull up to the curb. The brick house has two stories with multiple balconies and a three-car garage.

Sam parks on the street, among the other cars already there. "This is crazy," she says as we get out of the car. "You'd think a movie star lived here."

"To Chase, he *is* a movie star," I joke, and she laughs.

"What do his parents do again?"

"Dad's a lawyer, mom's a writer."

"Oohh, what kind of writer?"

I think back to our conversation downtown and remember how awkward he was about what she wrote, so I say, "I don't know," and leave it at that. That's for him to tell.

There's a note on the front door that says to head to

the backyard, so we walk around to the open fence and see the biggest backyard in the world. There's a giant pool in the middle, a basketball court, a trampoline, and still more grassy area. "Rich" isn't how I'd describe his family. "Extremely wealthy" is more like it. I suddenly feel uncomfortable and self-conscious. Like everyone can see that my old black dress and scuffed-up ballet flats I'm wearing are from a thrift store. The fact that I don't own a thing that's designer. That my entire house is the size of Chase's pool house.

"Penelope," I hear through the crowd of people—most of which are from our program. I turn to my left to see Chase. He's holding a red Solo cup and looking really good in dark blue jeans and a black button-down shirt. I look down at my dress again and feel frumpy.

"Hey, Chase," I say.

"Hey, Chase!" Sam bubbles up next to me.

"Come on, let's get you drinks."

I'm about to say I don't drink, but I follow him over to the bar out of curiosity. He gives Sam and me empty cups and says, "Help yourself," while gesturing to the bottles on the counter. I have no idea what to make of it, what to drink, so I glance at Sam, who looks just as confused.

"Beer is fine," she says smoothly, and I agree. Chase pours it into our cups.

"Hey, Chase," a voice calls, and he excuses himself.

"Can I be honest with you? I had no idea what to drink,"

Sam says, loudly whispering over the music playing off speakers closer to the house.

"Oh my god, same here," I agree. "I've actually never really drank before."

"Same! I don't even know if I want this. But I couldn't look pathetic." I smile at Sam, happy to have met someone like me.

"Yeah," I say. "Exactly."

Something grabs her attention at the gate behind me. Her face reddens and she looks away.

"What's going on?"

"*Nothing*," she says, so I look over my shoulder to see Jackson walking in.

"I *knew* it!" I exclaim.

"Knew what?" she asks, playing innocent.

"That there was something going on between you two."

"There's nothing going on between us," she says. "I totally think he's cute, but I don't think he's into me."

"Uh-huh. I seem to recall a tickle fight or something on the couch."

"Yeah, yeah, yeah," she says. "And what about you and Chase?"

My face must match hers, as I heat up. "One more time, it's nothing, we're just friends."

"Yep, friends, suuuuuure."

"I HAVE A BOYFRIEND!" I shout.

"Who I still haven't met!"

"You will, you will," I say, nodding my head, wondering where he's working tonight. I wonder how he'd react to Sam and Jackson. And Chase.

"Ladies," a voice says, and I turn as Jackson puts his arms around both of us. "Here's the thing—I was forced to come to this party and not sleep, like I really want to be doing, so let's make this exciting."

I can tell Sam likes him because she's not reacting. She's just kind of stammering, so I ask, "And how can we do that?"

"We toast," he says, holding his drink over my shoulder, in front of me. I lift my cup up to his, and Sam does the same. I notice that his free hand is over her shoulder, rubbing her upper arm a little. "To theater!"

Before I take a sip I hear, "Penny?"

It's a voice I'd know anywhere. A voice I can tell from miles upon miles away. A voice I'm usually thrilled to hear, but tonight . . .

"Logan?" I say, turning around and pushing Jackson's arm off. Later than I should have, I lower my drink. He'd die if he saw me drinking after his dad's drinking problem and all.

"Hi," he says, confused, looking lost and alone. He's rubbing his head, and kind of wobbling from foot to foot. "What're you . . . I didn't know . . ."

"Um," I say, knowing that everyone is looking at him and me. I step away from Sam and Jackson and take Logan by the arm. "What're you doing here?"

"Bounce house," he says, signaling over his shoulder at a bounce house that Chase apparently rented. "You know these people?"

"Yeah, acting-camp friends," I say, stopping our walk. We're away from everyone else now, on the other side of the lawn. I see Chase looking at us, so I look away. "This is Chase's house. Remember, I told you about the party?" I ask, then continue awkwardly. "I'm here with Sam? She's over there, the girl who I was talking to."

"And the guy?" he asks.

"Jackson," I say. "Why?"

"Just wondering."

"It's nothing to be worried about; you don't have to be jealous," I say, thinking of what Faye mentioned. "I mean—"

"Jealous?" he asks. "Who said I was jealous?"

"No one, I just . . . never mind," I say.

He breathes loudly and looks down. He looks so sad, so I touch his hand. Then he asks, "So, you gonna introduce me to your friends?"

My heart clenches. "Um, yeah, sure."

"Yeah? Sure? Penny . . . What's going on?"

"Nothing. I'm just having fun."

He picks up my cup and smells it. And by the look on his face, you'd think I slapped him.

"I wasn't drinking. I was just holding it."

"This isn't you, in a short skirt and drinking at some dude's party. Without me."

His words hit just as he intended them to. "I invited you!" I nearly yell.

"And I had to work."

"So just because you're working means I can't go out and have fun?"

He sighs and brushes his hair back, frustrated. "No, of course you can. You're just, I don't know, different here and I didn't expect that."

"That's why I haven't introduced you!" It comes out before I intend it to and I realize what I said as I watch his face change. "I mean . . ."

"No, that's fine. You didn't introduce me to your friends because you're a different person now, or whatever. You're embarrassed by small-town Logan. I don't have a freaking mansion or a plan to star on Broadway. So I'm not good enough all of a sudden? A few weeks at your new fancy camp and you're suddenly somebody else?"

I clench my fists beside me. "No, stop it, Logan. That's not what I meant. Of course you're good enough. It's me. I'm just . . . I'm maybe not that other person."

"What the hell does that mean? What is going on with you?"

"Nothing is going on," I say, unsure where the conversation is going and how we got here. I sigh. "I'm just having fun with my friends."

"With your friends. Sure. Go ahead and have fun. You clearly don't need me right now."

"I don't need you being jealous and insecure all the time. Just because I'm having fun without you doesn't mean I don't like you."

He pauses to look at me. "Don't like me or don't love me?" He walks away and every emotion hits me at once. Pain that we fought and longing to go to him. Relief that he's walking away and a desire to go back to my friends. And guilt. So much guilt. I look down and try not to cry.

"Hey, you okay?" I look up and Sam is next to me looking concerned. And for a second, a flash, I wish she were Faye. Faye would know what to do. "Was that Logan? What's he doing here?"

"He works for the bounce-house company," I say, pointing to him. "I didn't know he was coming."

"Didn't he know about the party?" she asks.

"Yeah, but I didn't tell him where it was or anything, since he couldn't come."

"Oh," she says. "Awkward."

"Yeah." I nod. "Really awkward." She keeps looking at me with sad eyes, so I try to smile, but it doesn't work. "I'll be right back," I say, heading out, away from everyone. I walk across the yard toward the lake and find myself by the boathouse. I look back and see everyone hanging out, laughing and dancing. I see Logan by the bounce house, testing it out. Even from here I can tell he's in pain. And it's all my fault.

"Hiding?"

"Oh!" I jump and find Chase looking at me.

"Are you hiding from someone?" he asks again.

"I'm not hiding," I say. "I'm just taking a break."

"From someone." He crosses his arms and leans against the boathouse.

"From everything."

"I think that's actually the start of one of my mom's books," he says, looking up, as if to remember. "The lonely girl walks off to the boathouse when the handsome sailor comes to rescue her."

"Because her boat sprung a leak and she can't swim back," I add.

"So he has to jam the leak. And then jam her."

"Oh god, that was awful," I say, chuckling, but not really feeling it. I look in the distance and see Logan turning around, presumably looking for me. And I feel guilty all over again for everything I said to him, and everything I'm doing now. Getting away from him, not dealing with it. For being here with Chase, and not there with him. "Thanks."

"For what?" Chase asks.

"For reminding me that I can fix my own leak without a sailor."

"I'm not sure how you got that out of the story, but go for it. Jam your own leak."

"Oh, ugh, I didn't—never mind," I laugh.

"Was that your boyfriend you were talking to?"

I tilt my head at his observation. I guess he could have guessed it by how we were talking. By the fact that he doesn't go to our camp, and Chase knew that Logan worked at a bounce-house place. Which makes me wonder. "Did you know Logan would be here?"

"Who's Logan?" he asks, genuinely confused.

"My boyfriend ..."

"Oh, no. No clue. I just hired a place. Coincidence, I guess."

"Yeah ..." And, for some reason, just like that, I find myself talking. "We're in a weird place, I guess. And I'm trying to figure it out."

"See, this is why I don't do relationships. Too much drama."

"No, you don't do relationships because you'll be tied down," I joke, not sure if it's true, but I'd believe it if it was.

"I'll give you that." He grins and leans back onto the boathouse, crossing his arms. "No, I wouldn't say I'm a love expert, but I've learned a lot."

"I really don't want details."

"No, from my mom."

"Wait, what?"

"No! God," he says, jumping up. "Her books. Her books. I think I just had a heart attack."

I smile. "Wait, you read your mom's novels?"

He shrugs. "Some. I'm curious, okay?"

I cross my arms and ask, "So, what have you learned?"

He sighs and leans back against the wall, letting it hold all of his weight. His black shirt is unbuttoned, showing a white undershirt untucked over jeans. When he reaches up, his shirt goes just high enough. "That girls want sailors to plug their holes."

"Oh my god," I laugh with him.

"No, and that, like, relationships are struggles. People change. And you have to decide if you want to change with them and become something new, or split. That's, like, the plot of all her novels."

I'm still laughing, but I get what he's saying. "I may have to read one of your mom's books now."

"I can get you a copy. Tell me, do you prefer firefighter, lawyer, warrior, king . . ."

"Yeah, yeah, yeah." I look at him and smile. "Thanks."

"Anytime. If you're in need, I can always help." He grins, leaning next to me with one arm propped against the wall. And I know he's not talking about advice.

"No," I laugh, pushing his arm, but he doesn't move. And neither do his eyes, which are staring down at me. I glance down, away, and then back, and he's still looking. And the way he's staring at me makes me want to move closer. How he gets me, how he holds the hope and promise of something new. How he's not looking away from me.

I want to kiss him.

Logan.

I break my gaze and glance over Chase's shoulder to see a few girls from camp looking at us, but mostly him. "I think you have plenty of damsels in distress waiting for you to help them with their leaks," I say softly, with a smile.

He shakes his head and turns around. When he looks back at me, he's grinning. "I guess I should set sail."

"You do that," I say, feeling relief we didn't do anything. Relief and also . . . regret. But I shake that feeling away.

He winks at me, turns away, and says, "Stop hiding, Penelope."

"It's Penny," I yell back with a smile, then turn to walk off. It's so much easier with him, where everything is fun and possible and open. But . . . there's also Logan. My Logan. I go to him.

His back is turned to me when I finally approach him.

"Hey," I say, and he turns around.

"Hey," he says.

"Let's go," I say, taking his hand and moving him through the crowd. He doesn't put up a fight, doesn't say anything, just lets me lead.

I want to get to a more secluded place so we can talk, but I see Sam, giggling next to Jackson, and backtrack. Maybe it was talking to Chase that gave me the boost, but I know what I want to do, at least right now. We walk up to them.

"Sam, this is Logan, my boyfriend."

"Oh!" she says, surprised, looking back and forth between the two of us. She probably senses the tension. "Hi! So nice to finally meet you!"

"Hey," he says uncomfortably, looking at me with curious eyes. I know these aren't the best circumstances under which to introduce them, but I'm trying. And I think he gets that.

"We're gonna head out in a bit, but I wanted you guys to finally meet, you know? And, oh, this is Jackson."

"Hey, man." Jackson nods his head and they fist bump.

I force a smile, then lead Logan away again.

"That was pretty awkward," Logan says as we walk.

"Sorry," I say. "I just . . . I'm trying."

He stops and turns me around. "What's going on, Pen?" There's a little white gazebo a few feet away, so I pull him inside, sitting down on the white iron bench.

"I don't know." I shake my head. "I feel awful for what happened earlier. I didn't mean it all, promise."

"Yeah," he sighs. "I think I know that."

"Think?"

"Do we have to get into this now? When we're at some dude's house?" He scratches the back of his neck uncomfortably, and I pull his hand down, placing it in mine.

"I'm sorry," I say.

He nods. "I *was* jealous."

"Of what?"

"Of this whole new life you have with all these new friends. I was kind of . . . surprised, I guess, to see you here. And then you were so comfortable with them, like they've been your friends forever."

"Just because I have other friends doesn't mean I care about you less."

"I know, I know. I just didn't . . . I don't know, I was surprised. And then you acted so . . ."

"Awful."

"No, different," he sighs. "I guess I thought you and I were enough."

I think about what I'm going to say before actually saying it. It's time to talk to him. It's time to finally admit what I've been feeling. All the confusion, all the distance. "I love you."

"I love you, too," he says, somewhat confused.

"I'm saying that because it's true. And because I want you to know it. But . . ." I start. I take a deep breath. "When we got together, I thought everything was perfect. I had, like, this tiny perfect world with you. I was in love with my best friend. And everything was . . ."

"Great," he says.

"Yeah . . . and we had this tiny future planned together, and, I don't know, I loved it. And I still do. But now . . . I don't know, I'm second-guessing."

"Me?"

"Not you. Not us. Just . . . here."

"I thought you wanted to go to college here. Then manage your mom's place."

"I do. I did. I don't know. Even my dad—my dad told me to do what I want, and not, like, rely on what's expected."

"I get it. I mean, he kind of ended up with the business. It wasn't his first choice."

"Right, so I don't think he wants that for me."

"So where does that leave you? And us?"

I shake my head. "I don't know."

He looks down, studies our hands, then looks back up. "And this has to do with camp, too, yeah?"

"Yeah. I mean, I'm in this school where people are planning on moving places, and doing big things. And it all sounds so exciting. And possible."

He looks up at me cautiously. "You know I'm staying here. I have to . . . and want to."

"I know."

"So what's that mean?"

"I don't know," I admit honestly.

He's quiet, then says, "My mom has a new boyfriend. He's a total douche, but she likes him."

"Where'd that come from?" I ask.

"I don't know—I want to change the subject."

I nod. "He's that bad?

"He wears a ton of cologne and has a goatee. Who actually has one of those nowadays?"

"Douches," I say.

"I can't believe you said that," he laughs. "So, yeah, things aren't perfect for me, either. I have a crap job that keeps me from practicing baseball, when not working I'm babysitting Mikey, and my mom relies on me, and yet she's also totally into a weird guy."

"I'm sorry." I lean on him and he puts his arm around me. I think of what Chase said and wonder, *Can we change together?*

We're not perfect—far from it. I think of one of the lines from the play, "an illusion of truth." We're like that. We're figuring ourselves out, and in that time turning into something new. We were like my character's unicorn when we started—a creature that was wonderful and ideal . . . and fake. Now our horn broke off. Now we're just a horse. And we have to get used to it.

I really hope we can.

EIGHTEEN

When I wake up the next morning it's after ten. I stretch and look at the ceiling, thinking of everything, but especially Logan.

I think he and I needed that . . . confrontation. It was so easy to be honest before we were dating. Now, every moment means something. There's so much more pressure on everything, and I can't hold it all.

My mind flashes to my dad. He's been out most nights and weekends, going to soccer games, going on dates. I feel a pit in my stomach like I'm missing something.

I grab a shower and get dressed and head over to the café. I pass a tiny coffee shop he and I used to go to all the time when I was little, before Mom died. We used to get hot cocoa if it was cold out. He'd wrap me in a scarf, even though I didn't need one because it was Florida, and put on my tiny blue gloves. I loved those mornings.

The last time we went was the day after I was accepted into camp. We got bagels and planned all the shows I'd be in. It was only a couple of months ago, but it feels like forever.

◇◇◇◇

I head inside the restaurant, the bell ringing as I open the door, and it's busy, as always on the weekend. I smile, thinking Dad'll be pleased. The new business nearby may be doing well, but you can't dismiss the local charm of our old place. The hostess waves hi.

"Good morning," I say, looking around. Every wooden booth is taken with people shoveling food down. Pancakes, yeah, but also eggs, waffles, bacon. A toddler holds up a bagel half and smudges cream cheese all over her face. I'm instantly regretting the apple I ate, and wondering if I could sneak something from the kitchen.

"Packed," she says, shaking her head so her blond ponytail whips around. "I don't know, something about today. People really want pancakes," she answers.

"That's not a bad thing!" I smile and look around.

"Your dad's in the back. I think a vendor is here."

"On a weekend?" I ask, and she shrugs.

The kitchen is in full steam, our head chef—a woman Mom hired personally—is mixing a giant vat of pancake mix. She has a few assistants assembling the plates, putting the food together, and scrambling the eggs. I wave and head through the side door to a small hallway that leads to my dad's office.

The door is slightly ajar, so I push it open with a "Hey, Dad!" and stop in my tracks. Dad is talking with a guy who may be a vendor, but the vendor is definitely sitting close and holding my dad's hand.

He's holding my dad's hand.

"Uh . . ." is all I manage to get out before I turn around and walk out. I think I hear my name. I think he's calling me, but I move in the direction I came. I'm in a fog and I can't think, can't think, can't think.

What just happened?

I get outside and just as I'm about to walk up the road, a hand grabs my shoulder.

"Penny, wait," Dad says, turning me around to him. He looks shaken, his hair standing up, his eyes wild, darting back and forth but always landing on mine. And I have no clue what I look like, or how I feel.

"Penny." He puts both hands on my shoulders, but must rethink, because he takes them away, and kind of paces around. He finally looks at me again and asks, "What are you thinking?"

"I . . . don't know," I answer honestly.

"This isn't . . . Dammit, this isn't how I wanted . . . okay, okay," he says, still moving around. "Can we . . . Let's go home."

"Dad, no." I shake my head. "You're here; it's the middle of the day. They need you."

"I know, I just . . . No, you're more important. Let's go."

"Dad, it's okay," I say. I don't know what else to say right now, what to think. What am I supposed to say? My dad was holding another guy's hand. Does that mean . . . ?

I flash back and see them together, leaning in. Sharing a joke maybe. Like they've known each other forever. Maybe he's been going out with him at night. And it hits me—he's never been specific. He said he was dating someone, but he never said *girlfriend*. I just assumed that.

Why didn't he tell me? I look at him, and he looks lost, rejected, and, I don't know, somehow, relieved.

"We'll talk later," I say, looking down.

"Are you okay?"

"Yeah . . . of course," I say. "Are you?"

"Yeah." he nods. "Yeah. I'm just . . . I mean, it's a lot for you and me and—"

"I know. I . . . I'm just surprised. Not in a bad way, in a . . . surprised way. It's not a bad thing," I reassure him, adding a small smile. "I just have a lot to process. We'll talk after work, promise."

With a relieved sigh, he hugs me, squeezes me tight, and walks back in. I know I should stay and talk, I know I should hear more, but seeing the relief in his eyes, and not knowing what to say . . . I just need to walk away for a minute.

I walk past a guy selling strawberries in a cart on the side of the road. Next to him, a little girl draws a sign to advertise. I smile and keep walking, but the guy and his daughter remind me of something.

The guy who was with my dad, he looked familiar. He looked like the guy Faye babysits for. The one with the daughter. Is it the same person? And if so, does Faye know?

I call Faye.

She doesn't answer, and I'm not sure if I'm more disappointed or relieved. I had no idea what to say to her anyway.

I find myself walking to the woods, where Logan and I hang out. I should call him, talk to him, but after last night I'm not ready, I guess. I sit on the fallen tree and rest my head on my arms.

My phone rings and I jump at the vibration. I look at it . . . and it's Sam.

"Hey," I say, my voice wobbly.

"Hi! What's wrong?"

"How'd you know something's wrong?" I ask.

"I don't know . . . Are things okay with Logan?"

"Oh," I say. "He's fine."

"Good . . . It seemed kind of . . . tense last night."

"Yeah," I say. "It's okay now."

"Okay, good. Glad I finally got to meet him!"

"Yeah," I say half-heartedly. I'm not really sure why I picked up the phone. I don't want to talk about all of this right now.

"What're you doing? Do you want to hang out?"

"Oh," I say. "Sure, yeah, that sounds good."

"Great! What do you want to do?"

"Anything," I say. "It's one of those mornings."

"Gotcha," she says, then promises to be here in thirty minutes.

She arrives in twenty-nine. By then I've walked back home; showered, wiping clean my thoughts; changed into shorts and a T-shirt; and left for the library.

Sam meets me in the theater section.

"I haven't been to this branch! I'm usually at mine; it's, like, five minutes away from where I live." I smile, knowing that, of course, Sam would be the only other person who likes hanging out at the library. I must not respond, because she says, "Okay, so let's talk."

"Ha," I say. I put down the Neil Simon anthology I'm holding. "Actually, can we drive around?"

"Of course," she says, not asking why I need to move, not asking where we should go.

We get in her car, and at the same time we both put our windows down. I put my hand out the window and feel the wind with my fingers. It's hot, but I let the road take my thoughts away, out the window and into the world. I let it all just fly away.

We drive around for about twenty minutes. Sam doesn't talk, and that's exactly what I wanted. But then she says, "Oh my god, what is that?" We pass the World's Largest Fake

Alligator. And seeing it—the place Logan took me—makes me cry.

"Penny? Oh my gosh, what's wrong?"

"Nothing, I'm fine," I say through tears.

"No, you're not. Hold on, I'll park."

She pulls into the alligator place and that just makes me cry harder. For Logan, and for not having Logan the way he wants me to. For my dad. For not knowing. For everything.

I know I need to explain myself, but I can't seem to find the words that encompass all of that, so instead I slip out, "My dad is gay."

And then I stop crying. And then I start again because I said it out loud. And she's the first person I told.

She looks at me and says, "Oh, wow, okay. Did you just find out or something?"

I nod because I can't respond.

"Are you okay with it?"

"It's my dad! And I literally just kind of found out! I saw him."

"Wait, with a guy?"

"Yeah."

"Oh, no, no, no. I never want to see my parents together. Ugh. Gross."

I look up and shake my head. "No, no, not like *that*."

She sighs and nervously laughs, and says, "Ohhh, phew. Because that's traumatizing. I saw my mom kiss her boyfriend once and wanted to bleach my eyes out. So what *did* you see?"

"They were just holding hands, and . . . I don't know. That's it."

"Still awkward. What'd your dad say when you saw?"

I sigh. "I probably could have handled it better. I was just . . . kind of a mess of thoughts. I left and he followed me out and . . . he just made sure I was okay."

"Are you?" she asks.

I shrug. "I will be. But I just don't get it. He was married to my mom for so long. I just wish I knew."

"Oh yeah?" she asks, and I realize I never told her much about my family.

"Yeah. They were so happy. And he still talks about her, and I know he still loves her. I mean, I know that you can love both guys and girls, I'm not stupid, but, I don't know, I guess I never thought that was my dad."

"It's not . . . a bad thing," she ventures.

"No, of course it isn't. It's just . . . It's something to get used to, I guess. I'd just heard he had a girl—er—boyfriend, I guess, and that was new. And now it's just something else. It's just, I guess it's not what I expected." I pause. "I mean, I'm happy for him and all, but it's a lot to take in. Seeing some-one in a different light. Not that *he's* different, but . . . Ugh, sorry, that was a lot to drop on you in one morning."

"It's okay." She smiles. "I'm here for you."

I sigh and think of my dad, and what I'll say. And what I'm doing in general. "I've been a bit distracted lately, honestly."

"Sounds like you need another night of adventure," she says and, for some reason, her phrasing reminds me of something.

"Remember those Choose Your Own Adventure books? Where you'd choose which way you wanted the story to go—if Bobby goes to the park, go to page five; if he goes home, go to page seventeen?"

"Yeah! Totally. I think my character always died or something. I never got to the 'real' ending."

"Exactly! So I used to do it right—just read along, but my friend Faye would always cheat—you know, flip ahead and see if she liked where the story went, then go back and change her answer if she didn't. She liked to know and I think that's because she always knew where she'd end up."

"Okay . . ."

"I wish I could pull a Faye right now and flip to the back and see what to do next."

"About your dad?"

"No, I love him. I mean, of course I do. I was just surprised. And sad he didn't tell me sooner. No, I just mean in general."

"But doesn't that take the fun out of, like, living?" she asks. "I don't know . . . I like not knowing. I like wondering and hoping. Being excited."

I think about what she said, and I love all that, too. But I also like to know. But the debate is pointless, because there is no book like that. Just hope. A lot of hope.

We go to lunch at a small sandwich place that's been in town for years. We sit on iron benches and eat egg salad sandwiches with pickle spears. There's a jukebox playing folksy music, and it's not ironic. And we talk—about everything. Then Sam takes me home.

"Thank you for today. For listening," I say. She hugs me and I get out of the car. It's the first time I really opened up a lot to her, and I'm so happy I did. I don't know what'll happen after the summer, but I know I'm glad I have her. Because sometimes you need someone to be grounded enough to pick you up when you need them. Sometimes you can't be perfect. Sometimes you just need someone to be there when you cry.

NINETEEN

When I close the front door, I jump when I see my dad sitting in the living room.

"Dad, jeez, sorry, I didn't know you were here."

He's folding his hands in his lap and says, "I came home after you left."

"Oh," I say, taking off my shoes and going into the living room. "Sorry, I went out with Sam."

He nods and is silent, and I don't know what to say.

"So," he starts after a few moments, and my heart thumps, "about what you saw. That's . . . that's Collin. And he's someone I've been seeing."

I breathe in and hold my breath, biting my lip. "Why didn't you tell me?"

"About Collin? There's . . . there's a lot to tell, and I

just didn't know how. Or when. I wanted to be sure, you know?"

"Yeah . . ."

"It's not what you expected, I know."

"No . . . I'm happy for you, that you are dating again. I am. It's just a lot to process, you know?"

"Yes, yeah, definitely," he says, leaning forward, relief pouring out of him. "And I'm here for that. You can ask me anything. It's still just me."

"I know." I nod. "I know. I just feel kind of in the dark and . . . left out. How long have you, uhh, known?"

"About . . ."

"About liking guys," I say solidly.

He sighs, rubs his face, looks away from me then back. "My whole life."

"Your whole life?" I nearly shout in shock. "And you still married Mom?"

"Honey, it's not . . . it's not a black-and-white thing for me. It's not either/or. I loved your mom very much—I still do, but that doesn't mean I wasn't also attracted to men."

"So . . . so you're bisexual?" I look at him quizzically, and then shake my head. "Sorry, this is so weird to talk about with you."

"It's okay, I know. It's awkward for me, too. Before, I never really . . . acted on it."

"Because of Mom? You were together in high school."

"Yes, exactly." He nods. "We've been together forever, it

feels. And I knew I was attracted to guys, but it didn't matter. I had her."

"So why . . . now?"

He sighs again. "It's not a decision, really. I mean, I guess it is—I can decide to not act on it, but that wouldn't be . . . it wouldn't feel right. If I'd found a woman I liked, I would have dated her. But I didn't. I found Collin."

"And you like him?"

He nods. "Very much."

I laugh nervously. "Here I thought I'd be weirded out the first time you brought a woman home. I wasn't expecting this."

He smiles and rubs my arm. "I wasn't, either. I'd like you to meet him, when you're ready."

"Yeah," I say. "I'd like that. I mean, how long have you even been . . ."

"Seeing him? Just a couple of weeks; not very long."

"I wish you'd told me."

"I know, I know. I just didn't know how. I was planning on it after your show. I didn't want to distract you. I guess . . . I blew that."

"It's okay."

He nervously looks up again. "I just . . . I just want you to know that I'm extremely happy with the life I've led so far. I loved your mother very much, and miss her every day. I'm so happy we had you. You're the best part of everything. I would never change a thing."

"Dad . . ." I say, my cheeks turning red.

"No, seriously. I want you to know, I don't regret anything. I'm happy with how everything turned out, and how I can live my life now. And I'm so happy we raised such a supportive, open-minded daughter."

"Can I ask—did Mom know?"

He nods. "I didn't keep anything from her."

"What'd she say?"

He smiles, looks away as if she's here in the room now. "She told me to not run away with Brad Pitt."

I laugh and hold his eye for a second.

"I love you, Dad."

"I love you, too."

◇◇◇◇

Dad leaves to work on some things at the restaurant, promising to come back so we can talk more. And I want that—I look forward to it. But in the meantime, I need to think.

I go to my room and flop on my bed. There's so much to take in and, again, I wish my mom were here. To talk it all out with. I can't believe she knew. And yet . . . I can. They were so close.

I take out her notepad again and keep flipping until I get to a blank page. I've never done this before, but I feel compelled to take out a pen, press it on the paper, and write.

Mom. I miss you so much. I remember her brushing my bangs back off my forehead. I can almost feel her doing it now.

I rub my eyes and realize I don't want to be inside. I want to move, I want to feel less restless. I grab my keys and head out. I look up at the house I grew up in, the house that's always been mine. It feels so encompassing, holding on to all of me. It feels like part of me, its roots sticking in. I shiver, then take a step forward, then another, then I run.

I'm not a runner, and realize it a few blocks in, when my breathing gets ragged and my side starts to pinch. But I keep going. I feel the pain and fight back to it. I want to feel it. I want to know pain and anger and fear. Tears drop from my face when I think of my dad figuring out how to tell me. When I think of Logan, and what we have. And Faye, my Faye, who I really need to see. I turn toward her street and rush up it.

There she is, at the end of the street. She's on her knees with two girls, drawing with chalk. My best friend.

She must sense me, or hear my breathing, because she turns around. Her eyes go wide, then soft, and her mouth makes an O shape. I've never seen her look emotional before—she doesn't do emotional—but I feel like it's coming on. She knows I know. She knows I know she knows.

I run up to her.

"Hey, girls, can you go grab the hula hoops from your driveway? I think we need them," she says, sending them away.

"'Kay!" one of the girls says, and then both run off,

skipping. I look at them and think of their innocence. I remember being that young. Everything was new and exciting and the biggest problem was being called last for the kickball team, or not being able to afford the latest trendy bracelet or something.

It all doesn't matter.

"So," Faye says, dusting her hands off on her shorts. She leaves streaks of pink and blue, and doesn't meet my eyes.

"You knew" is all I can gasp.

She nods her head, still not looking up.

"You knew and didn't tell me," I say.

"I couldn't," she says.

"You're my best friend!" I nearly shout, surprising myself with my outburst. And realizing how upset that makes me.

She looks up at me and shakes her head, eyes wide, signaling to the girls across the street.

"You're my best friend," I say again, whispering it. "We don't keep secrets from each other."

"This is different," she says, shaking her head. "This wasn't my secret."

"It became your secret!"

"Listen," she says. "No, it didn't. It was your dad's. How would you react if I told you your dad's secretly seeing a guy I babysit for? You'd never believe me. You'd be mad at me for telling you. You'd be mad at me for knowing before you. But mostly, you'd be mad he didn't tell you first. I know you would. I couldn't do something like that. I couldn't add to the anger and confusion you were already going to have."

"You could have hinted, or suggested . . ."

"What? What could I have said? 'Hey, Pen, ask your dad about that dude he's hanging out with a lot'? Sure, that wouldn't have been weird."

"But you knew!"

"And I knew you would soon, too."

"But—"

"Pen, I love you, and I wasn't going to be the person who changed your family. God, I would never do that. He had to tell you, not me. You know I'm right," she says, and I do, but that doesn't discount the fact that I'm mad at her. As if reading my mind, she adds, "And you're welcome to hate me. Just . . . can we talk about it first?"

I don't move. I just stare at the ground for a beat, finding my breath. Finding my thoughts. In time, I feel everything drain from me because she's right. I sit down next to her.

"How long have you known?" I ask.

"Not long. A few days, not even a week."

"Did he know you knew?"

"No," she says, shaking her head. "He came over one day when I was babysitting out here. I was going to say hi, but he looked really . . . I don't know . . . private about his conversation with Collin—the guy. Then he came back the next day. I didn't know for sure, but . . . I don't know.

You could sort of tell by how they interacted."

I shake my head in agreement. "I saw him with Collin, too."

"What? You did? When?"

"This morning. At the restaurant. I saw them talking, and I know what you're talking about. They looked . . ."

"Comfortable?"

"Yeah. And private."

"So, wait, he didn't tell you?"

"No, he did. I kind of caught them holding hands. Then we talked about it later, at home."

"How do you feel?"

I sigh. "I'm okay . . . now. I mean, I think I freaked out, I don't know. I saw Sam this morning, and she helped me."

"Sam?"

"She called at the right time, I guess. We went to lunch. I needed to talk to someone."

"You could have called me," she says a bit angrily.

"I did," I say.

She furrows her brow and then looks at her phone. "Oh. Oh. Shoot."

"Yeah," I say. "It was better I talked to her anyway. Since, you know."

"Oh . . . yeah . . . I guess," she says, looking down. I tap her sneaker with mine.

"I'm okay." I move on. "I really am."

"That's good," she says.

"You don't sound convinced."

"It's a lot to take in. I'd understand if you felt off."

"I guess I do, but I'm happy for him. I'm mostly upset he kept it all from me, like he didn't think I'd handle it. And it's weird him having a . . . boyfriend. It's weird he's seeing someone that's not Mom."

"Did your mom know?"

"Apparently, yeah. He said he never kept anything from her." I fill her in on more that my dad said.

Finally, she gives me a soft smile and says, "You know it'll be okay, right?'

"I do." I look at the girls playing and think of their parents. "Do you think people here will gossip about him? You know how small our town is."

"Yeah, but does that matter? You love him. That matters."

"I know it does, but I don't want him to be the talk of the city."

She shakes her head. "I don't know what to say. People suck, but hopefully they won't here. They know him. He's part of this community. They can't just turn on him."

I nod and look down, tracing some cracks in the sidewalk with my finger.

Faye gently puts her hand on my arm. "It'll be okay."

"This summer has been . . . wow."

"Yeah, it's been interesting."

"Why is that?"

"I don't know. Didn't we decide this is what growing up is all about? Dealing with this crap?"

"I don't like it."

"Yeah, me, either," she says, looking back at the girls. They're playing pirate. They're stealing gold and saving fair maidens. They're still living their tiny lives.

TWENTY

I don't leave Faye's, even though I know I should prob-
ably go back to Dad. But lying on the couch and watching
TV with her is so much easier. It takes my mind off things.
It reminds me of when this was all we did over the summer.

Faye's house is smaller than mine, and she has two older
brothers. They don't help out much, which is why it falls on
Faye's shoulders. She's tired, but she's tough.

Three hours into a movie marathon, her dad comes in
and grunts. He's in a white T-shirt and old jeans and smells
like beer. We quickly move down the hall and into her
room.

"Still no job?" I whisper as she shuts the door.

Faye shakes her head. "Nope."

"Ugh, sorry."

"Eh." She shrugs. "Used to it."

"Yeah, but now . . ."

"But now my mom still works, and I make sure she can buy groceries. Now I don't give him any money. Mom can do that. I support my mom and that's it."

"You know, you really should complain about your personal life more."

She smiles. "Not my style."

"How are you so cool?" I ask.

"Nature. Anyway. What do you want to do tonight? I'm assuming you're not going right home, since you've spent the day hiding out at my house."

"I have not been hiding out."

"Okay, how about recreational captivity?"

"Har-har."

"Any case, I don't want to stay here. Let's go somewhere. What's Logan up to?"

"Working. He texted me earlier."

"Did you tell him about . . ."

"Not yet. I wanted to do it in person." I pause. I think about hanging out at her house some more, or at Logan's house, or at any of the places we've been our whole lives, and feel claustrophobic. Then I think of the night out with Sam and Chase and feel . . . optimistic. "Let's go out. Somewhere cool, different, you know? Somewhere not . . ."

"Here?"

"Yeah."

"I don't know where. You've been going out with all your new cool drama friends."

"Hmmm," I say, thinking about what happened last night when Logan was involved. I look at my phone and see I have a text from Sam. She's checking on me, which is sweet. I let her know everything's fine, then casually ask if she's up to anything tonight.

Actually why I texted. Jackson having people over. Come?

I turn to Faye. "Hey, my friend from camp, Jackson, is having people over. Want to hang out with them?"

"Are they cool?"

"Jackson's nice. And Sam's awesome. She's so . . . She's kind of like you. But don't worry, you're cooler."

"That's what I want to hear. Where does he live?"

"Not far from here, but . . . we need a car."

Faye looks at her closed door, back to me, and smiles. "I've got an idea."

Twenty minutes later we're in Faye's dad's car. Her mom pays for the gas, and she gives her mom money, so she feels validated in us taking it. I don't complain. We're driving down the road, windows down, and it feels kind of freeing. Even just a few minutes into the drive and it feels like we're leaving the day behind. We're driving away, putting distance between us. And we need that. I need that.

I text Dad as we drive.

Going out with Faye. Will be home later tonight.

Then, because I don't want him to think I'm running
away from him, I add:

**Record soccer match and I'll watch with you. I won't even ask
about the offside rule. Love you lots.**

He responds quickly.

If you don't understand offside by now, you never will.

Then, like I did, a second later he adds:

I'll be happy to watch all the matches with you. Be home by midnight.
Pancakes in the morning. Love you.

I smile as we drive on. Dad may have someone new, but
he's still the same guy.

"I think we might be here," Faye says, slowing down the
car.

Jackson's house is in a typical suburban neighborhood
with similar-looking one-story houses, pretty trees in the

front yard, and wooden fences. It's the middle, between our area and Chase's. It's a happy medium, one I feel a bit more comfortable in. I'm not too out of place.

I'm wearing Faye's black shirt with my jean shorts, since I didn't really pack clothes when running to her house earlier. My red bow headband pulls my hair back. She's in a loose T-shirt and shorts, too. We really didn't prepare for a party.

There are several cars parked along the street, so I'm not surprised to hear lots of noise as we approach the door.

"Big guest list?"

Faye shrugs. "I hate parties. I'm one hundred percent doing this for you."

"I know, and I love you for it," I answer. I knock and Jackson answers.

"HEY-O, PENNY!" he shouts and I laugh because, judging by the glassy eyes, loud voice, and sloshing cup, I *think* he might have been drinking.

"Hey, Jackson." I smile, and he engulfs me in a hug. "This is my friend Faye."

"HEY-O, FAYE!" he says and hugs her. Her eyes widen and she stiffens at his touch. When he lets go, she physically relaxes. I suppress a laugh. "Sam is in the kitchen. She's making a punch that's so disgusting, but, hey, punch?"

"Are your parents out of town?" I ask.

"Yeah, took my sister to a dance competition today and they're staying overnight. So party!"

I shake my head and we walk in. There are more people here than I assumed. I know she said he was having people over, but I didn't think it would be like this—with people in every corner talking, and music blasting out of a speaker. I don't recognize everyone—a few are from our camp; others must be friends of his from school. I can feel Faye standing awkwardly beside me, so I turn to her and explain before I have a repeat of last night. "That was Jackson; he's in camp with me."

"I presumed. He's a hugger."

"He is. You loved it, didn't you?"

"Tremendously. Is everyone here from camp?"

"No, I only recognize a few people."

"So this should be a blast."

"Hmmm," I say, feeling awkward, too. I want to stay, I want to have fun, but I also feel bad that I made Faye come. This isn't exactly her scene; she doesn't normally socialize with strangers. "I'll tell you what. When you get bored, let me know and we'll leave."

"You'll probably be singing songs from your show by that point."

"You sound like Logan," I joke. "First, no songs because we're doing a drama. Also, I won't leave you. Let's have a code word. When we say that, it means it's go time. You can't argue with a code word."

"You're ridiculous," she says, then, "Marco Polo."

"Marco Polo?"

"I don't know. I've been playing games with kids all summer."

"Okay. Marco Polo it is."

"Marco Polo?" a familiar voice asks, and I turn around to see Sam. She's in jeans and a cute vintage-looking polka-dot tank top.

"Sam!" I say, not answering her question. "Thanks for inviting us."

"Of course! It's like, half our people, and half Jackson's friends. But they all seem cool—they're coming to see our show!"

"Oh, awesome!"

"Is Marco Polo in it?" Faye whispers, and I elbow her in the side. "Faye, this is Sam. She has a lead in our show, and is supremely talented. Sam, Faye—my best friend."

"Any best friend of Penny's is a friend of mine!" Sam says. "You want some cake? I made cake."

Faye looks at her, then me, and says, "I like her. There's cake."

I shake my head and smile. There's a knock at the door. I turn around just in time to see Chase walk in. My stomach flips a little. The last time I saw him, we were joking about romance novels. Which, in retrospect, is extremely embarrassing.

"You okay?" Faye asks.

"Yeah," I say. "That's Chase. Chase is in my show, too."

I must have been staring because Chase comes over

with an amused look on his face.

"You snuck out of my party."

"Just had to take care of something."

"Or some*one*," he says, nodding suggestively.

"Ugh." I roll my eyes. "Um, this is my friend Faye. Faye, Chase."

"Hey," he says, then looks back at me. "How's everything?"

"Good, yeah, okay," I say, waving my hand. I know Faye is looking at me, and I probably look ridiculous flailing about, so I stop, smile, and panic. "Um, we heard about cake, so we're going to go get some."

I look at Sam, and she leads us all into the kitchen.

When we're out of earshot, Sam looks at me and asks, "No, seriously, how're you doing?"

"I'm fine," I say. "I wanted to get out, you know . . . just have a little fun without thinking about anything."

"Yeah. Okay, well, we'll have fun tonight."

"Woo. Fun," Faye says and I squint my eyes at her.

"OH! You should try my punch."

"MORE PUNCH!" Jackson yells, running in.

"What did you do to him?" I ask.

"I have no idea." She shakes her head. "He told me to make a punch, so I did. As you know, I have no clue what I'm doing. I apparently made it . . ."

"IT'S AWFUL," he says. "AND I LOVE IT." And then he leans over and kisses Sam on the cheek. She smiles bashfully while my eyes open wide and I grin. And just like that, he runs out.

"What just happened?" I ask.

"Nothing. Shut it."

"Sam's *in love!*" I taunt.

"Is she always like this?" Sam asks Faye.

"Pretty much."

"Guuuuuys," I say, happy that my friends are getting along.

"She's like an eager puppy," Faye continues. "Like, you kind of want her to calm down, but you also think she's just so cute."

"I'm not sure if that was an insult," I reply.

Jackson pops his head back in. "SAM, IS IT TIME FOR CAKE?!"

"Wow, he needs to calm down," Faye says, and I nod in agreement. "But I mirror his excitement on cake. Where is this cake?"

"Come with me, my dear!" Sam says, grabbing Faye's arm and taking her away. Faye looks back and I can tell she wants to be angry, but Sam is too nice to be angry at, really.

And just as they leave, Chase comes in and heads straight to the cups.

"What's going on there?"

"Don't ask," I say. "How was the rest of your party?"

"Good. Fine. Nothing too exciting. Someone got drunk and threw up in the gazebo, so that was gross."

"Ew, I was in there, too. Prevomit."

"So it wasn't you?" He looks at me jokingly.

"No, I can definitely say it was not me."

Sam pops her head in and says, "Hey! We're gonna play spin the bottle. You in?" she wiggles her eyebrows and I laugh.

"Boyfriend." I shake my head. "Is Jackson playing?"

"Maybe," she says, turning red. "Chase?"

"I'm cool," he says with a shake of his head.

"Suit yourself," she says, then turns to go.

"Wait!" I call and she turns back around. "Is Faye in there? Is she playing? She can't be playing."

"Um, you should look out here," Sam says. I lean my head back and Faye is in deep conversation with a guy I don't recognize. He's super tall and thin and kind of nerdy-looking, with freckles and short-cropped hair. She'd eat him up normally, but she seems into him, kind of. Her guard is down and she's talking animatedly. She looks like she's having fun.

"Who is he?" I ask.

"Jesse. He goes to my school. I think his cousin goes to our camp, so he ended up at the party. Anyway, he's tech crew. Does lights for the shows. Plays the drums. Gamer."

"Girlfriend?"

"Nope. Honestly, don't know if he's ever had one."

"I love Faye, but she can be a bit . . . strong-willed."

"He can keep up," she says. "He once stood up to a

teacher for shaming a girl about her leggings. He's good people."

"Then I won't worry." I smile. I look back in, and Faye turns around, as if sensing me. She gives me a raise of her eyebrows, and a quick glance at Jesse. And a smile. An actual smile. I don't want to interrupt them, so I smile back and turn around to Chase. "What should we do while they play spin the bottle?"

"I don't know. Take a walk?"

Sam goes back to the game, and I lead Chase outside through the back sliding glass door. I thought it was a simple neighborhood, but standing out here I realize that Jackson lives up against a vast lake.

"Oh, wow," I say. "It's pretty." The moon's reflection glitters in the middle of the dark lake. It's large, spreading out across the neighborhood with at least twenty houses surrounding it. Screened-in porches, gazebos, and sand pits all dot the outline. And lots of trees, looming down, with branches reaching into the water.

I can smell the night—clear with a hint of mist that I feel on my bare arms.

"Where to?"

I look at him in the dark and suddenly I feel exposed. "The water." I take off my shoes and run through the damp grass, feeling it tickle my feet, until I hit the edge where there's a wooden railing for boats to tie off on. I hold on to it and look down into the murky, dark waters. It's waving slowly; there's some life still awake in there.

I turn around and Chase is close, looking at me.

"How's your girlfriend?" I ask, hoping to ease the tension, and remind him of why nothing can happen.

And he sighs. "Which one?"

"Gross."

"Penelope, you know I'm just having fun."

"Penny, Penny, Penny," I respond. "My name is Penny." There's a loud silence between our words.

"How's your boyfriend?'

"He's good."

He nods, then looks out over the railing. "This is something I like better about here than Atlanta—the water. You're always by it." He seems reflective, pensive.

"Yeah, it's easy to forget stuff like this is here, since it's everywhere."

"Do you live by a lake, too?"

"Thankfully not."

"Why thankfully?" he asks.

"If I lived by a lake, there'd be a gator in my house at least once a day. They go from lake to lake. We've seen them on the street. At night you can listen for the bang, and that's gator hunting."

"Where do you live again?" he asks jokingly.

I look away. "It's not that bad. I mean, it's different, I guess, but it's not awful. The people are nice. And there's always a story to tell. We have bears, too. They escape sometimes from a state park. They've been in our backyard a bunch, which is why we don't have a good fence anymore." I didn't want to open up like this to him, but I find it easier in the dark. I find myself wanting to talk.

"The raccoons are the worst," I continue. "Because they mess up your house if they're not happy. They'll take out windows, I swear."

"Are there lions and tigers, too?"

"Shut up," I say, hitting him in the chest. He takes my hand away, then holds on to it. I should take it away, but I don't.

There's a splash in the water. I turn quickly and see two puffs of air emerge, some bubbles, and something rough and brown. Something big.

"Gator," I nearly yell, grabbing Chase's arm and running back. Heart in my throat, I hold on tight and remember all the other times I've escaped them. Run fast, don't slow down, don't lose track of them. I breathe deep and pull Chase tighter, but he's letting up.

"Chase," I yell, turning back to see the gator's progress, and he pulls me to a stop. I'm pulling him, but he's resisting. Why is he resisting?

"Penelope," he laughs. "It's okay."

"What?"

"Log," he says, pointing out to the water. "It's a log."

"But the bubbles," I gasp. "The steam."

"Probably a fish or something. Man, you really must

have seen them a lot if you react that quickly."

I stop and stare at him. I look at the water again and shake my head and start laughing.

"I know if I'm ever in an emergency, I'd want you there," he says, still grinning.

"I've outrun a few of them," I say. "God, I can't believe . . ." I start, breathing slow, trying to calm my heartbeat. "Sorry."

"Don't be sorry," he says. "If it *were* a gator, and you weren't here, I'd probably be eaten."

I look at him and finally smile, too. "Probably."

"Hey," he says, nudging me. He puts his arm around my shoulder and turns me to him. Maybe it's the adrenaline coursing through my veins, but I don't stop him. He puts his free hand on my waist and I don't stop him from doing that, either. He brings me so close that our bodies are touching, and I don't stop him again. He leans toward me. And I lean, too.

Logan.

I pull back quickly before I do something I'll regret. I stare at him, then look down. Oh god. My heart thumps louder, harder, bringing me back to the reality of tonight. The reality of my life. What was I doing?

Chase sighs and stands up, brushing his hands on his jeans. I stand, too, but don't meet his eyes. I just breathe heavily, repeatedly.

"You're a good person, Penelope," Chase says, then walks off, back to the house.

And I'm left shaking my head because, *No, no I'm not. I'm anything but.*

I start breathing fast, tears springing to my eyes. *What have I done?*

I have to get away. I run back to the house, straight to the bathroom. I want to leave. I need to leave. But I have to calm down first.

I look at myself in the mirror and see a mess of a person. Tears streaming down my face, hair blown back, sweat everywhere. I'm not me. I'm not the same girl I was at the beginning of summer. I'm someone new and not nearly where I was supposed to be.

I take a few deep breaths and splash water on my face. I close my eyes and calm my racing heart. I can do this. I'm an actor, after all.

I get out and see Faye on the couch next to the same guy—Jesse.

"Hey," I say. When she sees me, she can tell something's wrong. She squints her eyes, then opens them wide.

"Did I tell you that Marco Polo story?" she asks, and I sigh inwardly because she gets it.

"I want to hear this story," Jesse says.

"I'll tell you later," she says. "First I need to take Penny home. Call me?" she says, and I want to be surprised that she said that—want to be excited for her, but I'm too tired now. Too far gone.

We drive home in silence. She knows something is off,

but I don't want to tell her, not now. I can't. I'm embarrassed as is. When she drops me off, she says, "It can't be that bad. Nothing is unfixable."

"I know," I say. "I think."

When I get inside, the living room light is dimly on. I look in and my dad is waiting up for me. He's not even pretending to read a book. And I just cry.

"Oh, hey, honey, it's okay, it's okay," he says, rushing forward to hug me. And I let him. I let myself shake and sob in his arms.

"Do you want to talk about it?" he asks.

I shake my head no. "It's not about you," I get out. "It's me. I'm a mess."

"You're not a mess," he says, stroking my back. I feel like a kid again. I feel like I just fell off my bike and he's making it better. I feel like the time that kid called me ugly, and he's reassuring me that I'm not. I feel seen and wanted and loved.

And I need him to feel that way, too.

"I shouldn't be complaining. You need support right now, not me."

"I'm fine," he says, a dad always pushing off his pain for his daughter. "What's wrong with you?"

"I don't know," I say, shaking my head.

He lets go of me, then makes the *One second* gesture. While he goes to the kitchen, I take my shoes off and snuggle up on the couch in the living room. I wrap a blanket around myself even though it's not cold.

Dad comes in with two mugs of hot cocoa and I smile.

"I know this would have been easier with your mom. I hate that she's not here for you right now to help you with everything. And . . . what's going on."

"I'm okay," I lie.

"Are you?"

I hesitate. "I'm just . . . doubtful."

"About?"

I gesture with my arms all around me. "Everything."

He pauses. "Including me?"

"No! No, not you. Come on, Dad," I say. "Just, everything else. I sort of . . . I sort of made a mistake with Logan last night, and don't know how to fix it."

His eyes get large and his face turns dark. "What kind of mistake . . ." he asks with a shaky voice, and it takes me a second to realize what he's thinking.

"No! No, not that kind of mistake. Jeez." I shake my head. "I love Logan, I do, but that's it, you know? I'm not ready for something like that, and it feels like this town is pointing me in that direction. I've got my whole life planned out here, which is great and also . . . suffocating, I guess. I'm going to community college after school. Then I'm going to work at the restaurant until I take it over. Logan and I will be together forever. And I'm thankful for all of that— believe me, I know how lucky I am to at least *have* a plan. But it's . . . I feel like there's no room to breathe," I admit.

"Honey, we talked about this. I want you to do what

you want to do. I don't care about what you think you should do."

"But that's the thing—I don't know."

"You shouldn't have to. You're seventeen. You have time to decide all of that."

"It just feels like it's already decided and I have no room left."

"It's not as hard as you think. What part is it? Logan? School? The restaurant?"

I shake my head. "I don't know. All of it."

He tilts his head. "How long have you been feeling this way?"

"A while. Since camp started at least. I love acting. And I love how everyone has these big plans that are scary and fun. Like, they may fail, but they don't care. They want to try. And . . . I kind of just want to try."

"Do you want to be an actress?"

"I don't know. It's not even that. I just want to be able to make my own decision. And I get how lucky I am, that I even have this for me, for my future. I know not everyone has that. But . . . I don't know."

He looks at me, then stands up and grabs his laptop from the table. When he sits back down, he opens it up and shows me a picture of a college campus. "This is something that's been on my mind. A former colleague from grad school told me about a teaching position opening up in a year, when his coworker is retiring. It's up in north Florida."

"Oh, wow . . ." I say.

"I love the restaurant, and I love that it'll be yours one day. But it was left to me to run, and it's not the business I want. I've been staying with it for you."

"But I don't know if I want it. What if I don't?" I ask, and it's the question I've been meaning to vocalize this whole time.

"I was thinking . . ." he says, nodding his head. "I was thinking of hiring a new manager and watching it from afar. So you could go back to it in time, if you'd like. And if you decide to go in a completely different direction, we could sell it eventually. But I want it there for you to choose, when the time is right."

"You want to leave the restaurant?" I ask, and though I'm surprised, I'm also not. It wasn't his; he was just doing it. For me.

"I've wanted to for a bit. Like camp helped you figure yourself out, Collin helped me see that. He's much less secretive about his sexuality, and the town hasn't been the most hospitable to him."

"I've worried about that . . ." I admit. "For you."

"I'm not. The town knows me; at most they'll be disappointed, but it's still me. I just don't like that it's bad for Collin. And I don't want you to feel like you have to stay here, when there's so much more out there for you."

"You really think there is?"

He looks at me with a smile. "Pen, I know there is."

I breathe in and out. I look at my dad, laying it all out, telling me *everything*. He's being so honest and true. And he looks so small and scared. I love him so much right now. For all he's done, and all he's going to do. Because he's my dad. And no matter what, he'll always be that.

I lean in and give him a hug, and I feel a sigh escape from him. Things will be hard. Things will be different. But nothing will take him away from me. Nothing.

"We should talk more often," I say, and he laughs.

"You think?"

After we talk some more, and Dad falls asleep on the couch while we watch TV, I go to my room feeling more relieved than I have in a while. Dad wants to leave. It's weird thinking that, but right. It gives me the chance to leave, too. If I want. Which I think I do.

I think about everything that's happened the past few days, weeks, months. The summer wasn't what I envisioned at all. I thought it would be perfect, and everything exploded. But was it all for the worst?

I think about my dad and him being open about everything now. And I think about Chase and Sam, and how they know what they want. And I realize I need to be honest, too. Maybe that's what needs to happen next.

TWENTY-ONE

I don't sleep that night. Guilt overtakes my thoughts and I just stare at the ceiling thinking about the next thing I have to figure out—Logan. About what I didn't do, about what almost happened. And I feel sick.

When I leave for camp the next morning, instead of turning right to go to the bus stop, I turn left. I need a personal day and I know Logan is home because he's working the next few night shifts.

When he answers the door, his face goes through a range of emotions—surprise, confusion, embarrassment, excitement, all while he yells, "Hey!" He picks me up for a hug and pulls me inside. "I wasn't expecting you. Shouldn't you be at camp?"

"Skipped," I said. "Wanted to come see you."

"I like that," he says with a soft voice, and I know what he's thinking. Empty house. Just us. I can't have that.

"Hey, can we talk?"

He steps back and stares at me for a second. "I don't like the sound of that. What's up?"

"Couch?" I suggest, walking to it. He stays where he is, and it's then that I realize he's still in his pajamas—a T-shirt and sweatpants. His hair is messy; he has his glasses on. He's not at the top of his game, and I'm doing this to him. I feel awful. I'm not trying to be. I'm trying to be honest, but I know it won't come out that way. "Come on," I say, and he hesitantly joins me, not quite sitting within touching distance.

"What's going on?"

"I just . . . I wanted to talk."

"I thought we figured all this out the other night."

"We did, mostly," I say, playing with my cuticles. "But I think I was wrong." I take a deep breath. My heart is pounding. How do I do this? Do I tell him gently? Do I give it to him all at once? What am I even doing? "Last night—"

"Stop. What's going on? You're never like this. You always tell me what's on your mind. Lately you've been thoughtful and tactful. I know I'm not going to like what you have to say, so just say it."

"Okay," I sigh. "Last night Chase tried to kiss me."

He stares at me and puts his head in his hands and I start to cry because this is what I expected. "So you kissed someone else?"

"No! I stopped it. We didn't kiss." I pause. I could stop here, but I know it won't be completely honest. "But I considered it."

He looks up at me, but not directly at me. "Do you like him?"

"No. I mean, not like that. He's a friend, that's all."

"Then why?"

"I don't know." I cry.

"Yes, you do," he says, looking away. "You're ashamed of me. I get it."

"Logan," I say, reaching to him, but he moves away. "It's so not that—not at all. I love you. I do."

"Then why didn't you introduce me to your friends? It all makes sense."

"I did! I'm not embarrassed by you. I guess . . . it was dark, and we were alone, and . . ."

"Oh, good, that makes me feel better. That you'd go somewhere with some dude I don't know in the dark."

"We were just outside. Chase is . . . Chase is different."

"I really don't want to hear about him right now."

"No, it's not that. Chase wants to go star in movies. He wants to do big things."

"So he's better than me because of that. Because I'm just a guy who wants to stay home. I knew it would come back to that. I knew you weren't happy."

"I'm unhappy with myself, not you. Please believe me. I'm confused. Not about you, but about me." I pause. "I want to go on and do big things, too. I want to try."

"And I'm holding you back. Fine, go, Penny. Do what you want to do."

"Logan." I sniffle. "I know I don't deserve it, but listen to me for a second?" He crosses his arms, but he leans back. I've never seen him so upset. I've never seen him so heartbroken, and it's tearing me apart. If there's anything I want, it's for him to know it's not his fault. "I know it seems like it does, but it has nothing to do with you. I love you. I always have. You're my very best friend. But . . . hearing that we're staying here and making future plans *here* with marriage and kids . . . it started to freak me out. I KNOW you don't want all of that right now, but my life seemed so straightforward and planned out. No surprises. No risk. I've never wanted risk before, but maybe it's the camp—you're right— or maybe it's just me getting older. I want to try something crazy. I want to go somewhere. I want to figure out who I am outside of Christmas. I don't want to be stuck here forever. And I don't mean stuck here with you—that's not it at all. I'd take you anywhere. I just . . . I don't want to know what the future holds yet."

He shakes his head. "What do you want me to say to that?"

"I don't know. I just wanted you to see my side. I was with Chase because he was the unknown. I don't want him, but . . . I want the unknown in my life."

"We talked about this. You know I'm staying here after

graduation. You know I just want to settle down and all that boring stuff you mentioned after college."

"I know."

He breathes out. "So what about us?"

This is the hardest thing I'll have to say. I know it'll hurt him; I know it already hurts me thinking about it. "I think I need to be alone for a bit."

He gets up and paces. "So that's it?"

"I figured you'd want to break up after . . ."

"That's what you don't get. It may be boring, but I'm in it. I'm in it with you. I can get over the crappy parts."

"But I can't." I shake my head. "I need time to process the crappy parts. And myself. I just . . . I want to be me."

"So we're done?"

"We're . . . on hold?"

He shakes his head. "Whatever you say, Penny. Whatever you say." He says it, but I know in my heart he doesn't mean it. He's going to wait for me. He's loyal like that. And part of me wants him to—part of me really hopes one day we can be this happy family he wants. But not now. Part of me wants him to explore, too. Even though I'm terrified he'll meet someone else, someone who's willing to stick around. My heart already hurts thinking about it; I don't want to think about it. And maybe feeling that, knowing that, gives me pause. Gives me hope that there's a future for us.

"Maybe this is mean for me to say, but I have to say it. . . . I want there to be a future for us, I really do. I want us to be together one day. I just need this time, right now, to myself."

He shakes his head, and I've said too much. I've hurt him, and I know telling him there might be a future may be even worse. But I love him, and don't want to lose him forever. I can't.

TWENTY-TWO

The next day I go back to camp. Everything is normal, but it's not. I feel a little lower, a little less buoyed. And it's okay—it's just not something I'm used to. I'm sad.

I see Chase in the hallway. He's animatedly talking to a girl. I don't bother to see who it is. He raises an eyebrow at me, but I avert my eyes and keep walking. I don't want to deal with him now.

I see Sam and she asks me what happened, why I left the party early, and I tell her I wasn't feeling well. I have a feeling she'll figure it out when we start having lunch just the two of us. Or maybe I'll tell her. Just not now. I'm not ready for that yet.

Rehearsals go on for the next few weeks. I get more into the show, the character, and love every minute of it. It puts me in a different place, and I don't have to think about Logan at home. I just have to think about the moment.

I focus my free time on props. I practically sleep at the theater, throwing myself into it. I help build a kitchen table, and then decorate it with period place mats. I find a vase in the closet and polish it until it shines. I organize silverware on the table, as it should be. And I fit the menagerie onto its stand. In the end there are thirty pieces, over half actually glass. All shine. When they knock together, they're musical.

As I reread the script for probably the millionth time, I realize something—I'm not my character. I liked Laura because I felt like her—content in who she is. She has enough; she doesn't want more. She's delicate like her glass.

Then there's her brother, Tom, Chase's character, who wants *everything*. He wants to leave his dead-end life and see the world, like their father did. But it would mean leaving Laura behind, and that killed him. Still, he goes.

And still, I will, too.

My show comes and it feels surreal. I'm not in it the first night, but I still have nerves creeping through my body. All of the cast and crew gather around backstage standing in a circle, about an hour before we go on.

"Folks," Teresa starts. "I just want to say, I'm so proud of you. You've taken this show further than I could have imagined. I can't wait for tonight." There are cheers and fists in the air. Next to me, Sam, already in costume, throws her arms around me and squeezes.

"In the tradition of theater, it's time for the gypsy robe." I laugh because my school has one, too—a robe that has a piece of each show it's been handed down through. It's awarded to the person who's helped out the most, as chosen by the director. They get to wear it and then leave their mark. Teresa takes out a dark purple robe adorned with programs and flyers and ribbons and pieces of material and a little toy car, it looks like. It's a menagerie of fun.

"This robe has been with the Breakthrough Camp family since the beginning, and this year I'm happy to pass it on to the person who contributed the most both on the stage and off. Someone who not only understood her character, but understood the message of the play and showed it through her work. Someone whose determination helped bring the set to life. Someone who's shown the most growth as an actress. And that person is Penny."

I stop and stare wide-eyed as Sam squeezes tighter. Me?

"Come on up." Teresa smiles and I walk shakily. Everyone is cheering and clapping and, out of the corner of my eye, I see Chase give me a smile. I meet Teresa and she gives me a hug, whispering in my ear, "Thank you for all you've done, and all you've learned." She puts the extremely heavy robe on me, and I snuggle into it. This is when you're supposed to run around and let everyone see it, but instead I take in the moment. I close my eyes and feel the weight, the magic, the *everything* this cape represents. I let it all in.

And then my night comes. I stand in the dressing room, putting on my lipstick and concentrating on my character. Sam is doing a sound test, and I'm alone. A mix of feelings rumbles through me—I've led productions before, but this seems so much more professional, so much more meaningful. I let my nerves take over, and I smile.

There's a knock at the door and I say, "Come in," expecting a techie with my lapel microphone. But it's Chase.

"What're you doing here?" I ask.

He sits on the couch, arms on his knees, and takes me in. "You've been avoiding me."

"You noticed," I say, going back to my makeup.

"I shouldn't have tried to kiss you. I know you have a boyfriend. You reminded me. A lot."

"Had," I say with a sigh, then, "It's not you. In a weird way, it was probably good. It helped me see a lot of things."

"Yeah? Like how handsome I am?" he asks with a smile.

"You are so full of yourself." I shake my head. "I like acting, I really do. May not be as good as you or Sam, but I want to try. I think you were right. I've put up a wall to not let it in as much as I want to. Because I knew it wasn't my future, and didn't want to be too upset when it ended. But . . . I'm lowering it now. I want to try. I may never be a great Hollywood actress or anything, I may come right back here immediately, but . . . I want to try."

"Talking a big game now." He smiles. "I like it."

"Oh yeah?"

"Listen, I knew you had potential, you just wouldn't let yourself see it."

"And you know everything, huh?"

"Always." He smiles and I shake my head.

The door bangs open and Sam runs in. "HALF HOUR TIL—oh, hi, Chase, what're you doing here?"

"Giving ol' Penelope a pep talk," he says, standing up.

"Seriously, PENNY."

He winks at me and walks out. I look at Sam and say, "Before you even think it, no. I'm not going to end up with Chase. He's too cocky."

"I know, I know." She waves her hands in protest. "I wasn't hinting that. I actually get it."

"Good." I nod.

"Excited for tonight?"

"More than is possible, I think." I giggle.

"You're more than ready, that's for sure," she says. "Your dad coming?"

"Yeah, with Collin. It'll be the first time I see them out together—I mean, he's come over a few times, but, you know, out in public, and that'll be cool."

"So you like him?" she asks merrily.

"Yeah, definitely. He's really nice. And he really likes my dad."

Sam lies on the couch, fully in costume, and I worry she's going to wrinkle. "Anyone else coming?"

"Faye . . ." I stop because Logan was supposed to, too,

but I don't know. I don't know now. I don't deserve for him to come.

As if reading my mind, Sam says, "He'll be here."

"You think?"

"Yeah, I do. Now go get your costume on!"

Before the show, I walk onstage and help set up my menagerie. Even though I don't have to do my prop duties tonight, I still feel compelled to. It's still mine. I take an immense amount of pride in organizing the menagerie each night, making sure it's perfect. I find myself more excited about that—the details—than about acting sometimes.

When I pick up the tiny glass monkey, his arm drops to the ground. My breath hitches—it must have broken in the previous performance. The audience won't know he's lost an appendage, so it's okay, but still sad. I wrap him in my hand and touch his little head. He's no longer perfect, but he is usable. He's broken but not gone.

And then, as I finalize the setting, they yell for places.

As much as he annoyed me in the beginning, Chase did teach me a lot. And I use everything in my character: the openness to senses, the fear and excitement of not knowing what's coming next, the belief in what I'm doing, and the spontaneity of the moment. I channel all that as I walk onstage.

The curtain rises and Chase starts his monologue. We're mixing up the cast, and using two understudies and two cast people, just like we did in rehearsals. So I'm comforted seeing

Chase, and I'm thrilled seeing Sam, out there with me.

In the first scene, I'm sitting on the couch, organizing the glass pieces, just as I was moments ago. I put them in place, I move them around. I hold them up again. But I'm Laura now; I'm not Penny.

And in that moment, I remember something important about glass: it's delicate and clear, but if you hold it up to the light, there are a million beams that shine through. There's so much more to it. There's so much more to me. I'm not a perfect unicorn or a broken monkey. I'm still being designed, constructed. I'm exactly what Teresa said I was—a work in progress.

So when it's my turn to say my line, I don't miss my cue. I open my mouth. And I let out everything I want to say through Laura's words.

◇◇◇◇

As the applause rises and cheers bellow out, I stare out into the audience. I take a bow with the rest of the cast, the four of us holding hands tightly between one another. Jackson is to my right and he's laughing, and Sam is to my left and she's beaming. I'm exhausted and energized all in one. I'm on fire.

I steal a look into the audience and see my dad a few rows back with Collin and his daughter. She waves to the stage and holds up flowers. Dad is teary-eyed, I think. There's Faye on the other side of the room pumping her fists in the air, the most excited I've seen her in a while. And down the aisle, at the very end of the row at the back of the theater, is

Logan. I barely see him, but I know it's him. I can't tell if he's smiling or not. But he's here.

We take another bow and as the curtain falls, a cheer screams out of me as we all hug and celebrate a show well done. My first professional show. I can't stop smiling from the experience, and the feeling of being *seen* by so many people.

"All right!" Teresa cheers as we hug one another again and again. "Excellent job!" Sam holds on to my waist, and I close my eyes, remembering the moment always. "Go catch up with the audience—you've got quite the crowd waiting for you."

I don't wait a minute longer.

I run out and see Faye first. "There's my girl," she yells, and it's only then that I realize she's with Jesse from the party.

"Oh, hiiiii, Jesse," I say, giving Faye a wink, and she rolls her eyes.

"Don't mind her," she says to Jesse, and I give her a hug. Despite her hating it. So she picks me up and spins me around, and I squeeze her back.

My dad stays back, letting me have my moment, but I turn from Faye and run to him anyway.

"I'm so proud of you," he says into my ear as I wrap my arms around him. And the thing is—I'm proud of him, too.

"You were wonderful!" Collin says, giving me a hug, too. He's taller than dad, with light hair and light eyes and a kind smile. He's a good counterpart.

His daughter thrusts flowers into my arms and says, "You're famous!" I laugh and scoop her up.

I see Logan standing apart from everyone, and my heart jumps. I put her down and walk up to him nervously; more nervous than the time I had to apologize for hitting him with a baseball all those years ago.

"You came," I say breathlessly, and before he can respond, I add, "I miss you."

"I miss you, too," he says awkwardly, looking down. I hug him, and he hugs me back. We stay like that for a while, not moving, not letting time or space get to us. We're one within a big theater within a bigger city, within a big state. We have so much around us. But for now, we're enough.

I'm not the same person I was when I started this.

So when we break apart and look at each other, our faces light up.

"You're gonna do big things," he says with a hint of remorse in his voice.

"No, *we* are," I say. I need my time now, but when I look at Logan, I see a future for us in his eyes. Not right now, but someday. When he takes my hand in his, I know he sees it, too.

While everyone is still gathered outside, I sneak back into the auditorium. The noise from outside is vacuumed out as soon as the door shuts and I'm left in beautiful silence. It's empty and so different than it was just twenty minutes ago when I was on that stage and everything felt alive. *I* felt alive.

I don't know if I'm going to become a famous actress. I don't know if I even want to, but I know now that I want to try, and I want all the uncertainty that comes with it. I need to pick the future I want. I don't know where I'm headed, but that's okay; I like the mystery of it all. I don't want to turn to the back of the book and see the correct path to take to lead me to my perfect ending.

No, I want more than that. I want to make millions of decisions and revisions. I want to be right and wrong. I want to live in this delicious moment of uncertainty and see what happens next.

Acknowledgments

◇◇◇◇

To Karen Chaplin for your faith in me. For pushing my writing when I didn't know what to do. And for the phone call that made everything click (what if there was no mom?!?). To everyone at HarperTeen that worked their magic—Emily Rader (managing editorial); Olivia Russo (publicity); the entire sales team; and Bess Braswell, Tyler Breitfeller, and the rest of the marketing team. To Michelle Taormina for designing my amazing cover, and to Dmitriy Podessto Pogorelov for creating the STUNNING artwork. I'm in awe.

To Claire Anderson-Wheeler for all your help, all your care, and all that you do. For answering my long, rambling emails, even when they're not important. And to the entire Regal Hoffman team for being terrific.

To Misty White for reading, I don't know, a hundred drafts of this? For not hating my writing . . . yet. To Colure Caulfield, Michelle Carroll, and Megan Donnelly for being the best friends a girl could ask for. To Shannon Calloway for bringing my book around the world (literally). To Joe Chandler for writerly emails.

This book wouldn't have been possible if not for Jane Mueller, and for her instilling the love of theater in my ninth-grade mind. Thank you for giving me the best high school memories, and for believing in me. Go Troupe 2888! And thank you to Amanda Schlan for all the acting antics we got into as children. Oliver & Annie forever.

One of the best parts of being a writer is befriending other writers. Thank you to Jenny Torres Sanchez and Jessica Martinez for being my rocks, my backbones, my favorite people to vent to. To Jenn Marie Thorne, Kathryn Holmes, Sharon Huss Roat, and Eric Smith for, in order, all the chats, the fun car rides, the many emails, and the OMG texts.

To librarians everywhere—you are the real rock stars. (Specific shout-out to Alafaya Library and Team Meerkat.) To educators, thank you for doing what you do. To everyone who's had me at events, thank you. To bloggers for constant support. And to readers, THANK YOU for showing so much love. You have no idea how much it means to me.

To my parents for all their love and support. To my dad for ALWAYS being the first to read my books. To my mom for letting me watch *Grease* and taking me to see *RENT*, both when I was far too young, but man, did I love them. And for continuing to see shows with me now. To Justin for being Justin. And to Jetta.

To Samir for unwavering support and love. I couldn't do it all without you. And to Leila, for showing me every day how much I can love another person. To seeing millions and millions of banana moons together.

Turn the page for a peek at
LAUREN GIBALDI'S heartfelt novel.

ONE

FAMILY.

The word is big, bold, and blue on the whiteboard, underlined three times.

"Family," Ms. Webber, my photography teacher, says aloud, rolling the marker between her palms. "What does it mean to you? Who is in your family? How would you define family?" She looks around the classroom. "For your next photography assignment, I want to see your version of family."

I shift in my seat, the squeaking of the chair sounding as loud as a siren. I look around and see everyone nodding and starting to jot down notes. My paper is blank; I'm not sure what family means. Not really.

"When's it due?" Celine asks from the other side of the

room, pencil tapping on the table.

Ms. Webber answers, "December, so you have two months, but it's part of your final portfolio, so you'll be balancing daily classwork and other projects as well. This is your first long-term project, and I really want you to focus on it." She turns around and I swear she looks right at me. "I want you to impress me with it."

I breathe in deep and can't help but wonder if she knows how much this terrifies me.

"Okay, for the remainder of today's class, I want you to start planning your photos and how you'll present them—exhibit style, online, physical portfolio, et cetera. Go ahead and use the computers, or walk around for inspiration," she says.

As soon as she's done, chairs scrape the floor as they're pushed out, conversations start, and I'm still here, in my seat, frozen. Because I have no idea what I'm supposed to do, what I'm supposed to focus on.

I sit for a few more minutes, then start to get self-conscious. I don't want to look like I'm lost, so I head over to the editing bay—what we call the row of computers where we edit our photos—and look for the latest picture I'm working on for another assignment. It's a photo of a bike, left alone on the side of the road. It looks like it's been there a while, chain rusted and weather worn, and becoming part of the ground. I can lose myself in this project now, then figure out the family assignment later. I pull up Photoshop and get to work, changing the exposure and making the photo a little lighter, hoping to give it a more fantastical feel.

"So what do you think of the assignment?" Celine asks, sitting down next to me. Her slick dark hair is pulled into a low bun and I'm suddenly conscious of the frizz escaping my ponytail.

"I don't know yet," I admit, looking back to my computer. I've been in-class friends with Celine for three years, since starting photography my freshman year, but only this year, after my best friend, Treena, left for college, have we become closer. She knows why the subject makes me uncomfortable—I told her all about it over pizza after we had an assignment about secrets. Not that my adoption is a secret; it's just not something I reveal every day to people.

"You're gonna do it on your parents, right?"

"Yeah, of course," I say, clicking the mouse absentmindedly. "I mean, they *are* my family."

"I know, I know," she says, swishing her hand. "I was just wondering if you ever thought about, you know, your *real* parents."

Real parents. The words affect me more than they should.

Truth is, yes, *of course* I have. How could I not? I always wondered who the people were who gave me this frizzy hair, this bumpy nose. This penchant for biting my nails, and lactose intolerance. But I guess I never thought of them as family. Just, more as people who were part of my life long ago that I don't know or remember.

But I don't say all that. Instead I say, "A little, I guess" and leave it be. Because how can I describe the numerous Google searches without sounding just a little bit crazy? Treena understood, but that's because I've never kept anything from her, and she went through it all with me. But I don't want to go back there. "What about you?" I ask, changing the subject. "How are you going to fit in all seven hundred family members?" Unlike me, Celine has a *large* family of four siblings and numerous aunts and uncles and cousins.

"Ha," she says, opening up her own photo to edit. I look over and see a picture of a dog, and though it sounds simple, the lighting is really great and the dog's eyes shine. "I think I'll just focus on my parents and brothers and sisters. They're family enough. Did I tell you, my little brother tried to eat my last portfolio project? Like, I found it . . . in his mouth."

"Oh god. I can't imagine it tastes good."

"Mmmmm, photo paper." Celine chuckles and adjusts the lighting on her picture a little bit more. She's a better photographer and Photoshopper than me, by a lot. Sometimes I wish I had her talent. "Anyway, I'm going to Java Jump after school, want to join?"

"Yeah, maybe." I turn back to my computer screen and work on my photo some more. I don't know if I'm making it any better or worse; I'm just changing it to keep myself busy.

4

So when the bell finally rings, I quickly pack up my bag and start to head out.

"Maude." I look up and Ms. Webber is standing by her desk, smiling. "Can you come here for a second?" My heart thumps as I mentally retrace all of my assignments, wondering if I turned something in late. Celine gives me a devilish grin and gestures toward our teacher. She's used to being called up and reprimanded. Me . . . not so much.

When I get to her desk, she looks at the room, then back to me. I look around and see that most of the people have cleared out, except for a few still on the computers. We have a tendency to stay here during other classes. If she thinks we need it, Ms. Webber gives us an excused pass.

"I wanted to ask you if you've thought about the family assignment."

"A bit." I hate lying to her because she's nice and she's always here for us. She's younger than most of the other teachers, with bright red hair, brown glasses, and a stare that penetrates you until you confess all of your secrets.

She nods. "Look, I know this must be a harder assignment for you, but I also think it'll challenge you in ways other students won't understand. I think, because of that, it will make you a better photographer."

"You think?" I ask, a bit skeptical.

"Definitely. I just want you to know that I'm here, in case you have any questions."

"Thanks," I say, awkwardly adjusting my books in my

hands. "I don't really know where to start."

"You'll figure it out," she says with the conviction only a teacher who's seen it all can have. And, I don't know, I kind of believe her. "I also wanted to ask, have you started looking into colleges yet?"

"Not yet. I've looked at some pamphlets, but I haven't made any decisions. I think I might want to major in photography, but I don't know," I admit, because I do, but is that the right step to take? It's such a huge decision.

"Well, that's up to you, but if you *do* decide on that, I can definitely recommend a few colleges."

"It's not a bad major? Like, I could eventually get a job, or something?"

She nods. "I did, right?" She smiles. "You should do what makes you happy and what you have a talent for."

I smile back and thank her, then leave the classroom and head out to lunch. The rest of the day glides by, and I barely notice; I'm too wrapped up in my thoughts. After the final bell, I walk home. I don't live far, a few blocks, and I hope the walk can help clear my mind. Of the project. Of the future. Two girls from my trigonometry class wave to me, and as I wave back, a burst of fall air blows leaves across my feet. And the breeze feels good. It feels like a breath of something new.

◇◇◇◇

When I get home, I find a stack of college flyers in the mailbox. They've been coming in daily since junior year started.

Inside, I toss the mail on the kitchen counter and head

to my room. My laptop is already open, and I stare at it, thinking about photography class and my assignment and what Ms. Webber said. I walk over to my desk, wiggle my mouse, and Google "Claire Fullman."

It's one of the two bigger things I know about my birth mother—her name. It was a semi-open adoption, and my parents met her once, so they've given me that much information, along with whatever else they remembered—she was short and had dark, wavy hair (like mine). They'd planned to send her updates as I grew up, but then she died when I was born due to some sort of complication.

That's the second thing I know about her.

Once again, my search comes up with absolutely nothing. A few Facebook pages, a wedding photographer, white pages information, all for people very much alive. She lived before everyone documented their lives online, as my mom tried to explain the first time I unsuccessfully looked for her, but it's still frustrating. How can someone leave no footprint at all? How can a person have no impact? I try adding "Tallahassee" to the query, which is where I was born, but again come up with nothing. I add "Florida State University" because I know she went there, but again, nothing. I shouldn't be upset—I've done this dozens of times—but I still sigh and shut my computer, wishing my past was tangible.

I look up and see the photo pinned to my corkboard, showing my parents and me at my tenth birthday party.

They took me and a few friends ice-skating. In the picture my face is flushed from the cold, and my knees are red from ice burn, but I'm so happy. I'm squeezing my mom, and she's laughing because I'm taller than her in the skates.

I could do that. I could just take pictures of us, the three of us, together. Because they are family—they're my family. They're who raised me and helped me become, well, me. And I love them, of course.

But part of me knows that just showing them isn't enough. That I can show so much more if I try. I just don't know how to try.

My fingers twitch and I know I need to take my mind off this, get away from it for now. I might as well join Celine at Java Jump. I grab my camera from my bag and throw the strap over my neck. I feel more complete with it, like it was begging for me to pick it up.

I grab my keys and head out, wanting to make the most of the changing weather. I take a left out of my street, cross over the train tracks, and head north toward the shopping center on the corner. Cars pass, birds fly overhead, and the sun begins to consider setting. I love this time of evening.

Shouts and laughter tell me that there are kids playing at the nearby park. I stop and see parents sitting on the benches talking, no doubt comparing stories and woes. They're having their own, real-life conversations as a world of activity takes place right in front of them. There, spies are murdering dragons, princesses are being rescued by superheroes, and the evil villains are always captured no matter what. I lean against a post, just outside the sandy playground that holds a slide, swing set, monkey bars, and seesaw.

"Hi, Maude," one of the mothers says to me, and I smile and wave in response. I've babysat her daughter before. In fact, I've babysat a lot of the kids here. It's both a curse and comfort of living in a small suburb—we've all lived here forever, so we all know one another.

A little girl with bright red pigtails—the woman's daughter—is sitting at the top of the slide, contemplating her descent. She has a finger in her mouth, and a hand clutching the railing. My fingers twitch again, so I point my camera up and slowly adjust the lens to focus in on her, blurring the trees and houses behind her. I get absorbed in her world, feeling her worries, her pains, as I capture the moment. Everything looks so much better through the viewfinder. Easier and clearer.

She takes the finger out of her mouth and grabs the other bar. No one is behind her. She has all the time in the world. I click, showing her slow resolve. Then, with a slight push, she slowly totters down the slide, slipping, slipping, slipping until she gets to the bottom with a laugh of excitement. I shoot everything, the determination in her face, the change from fear to joy, the cry of happiness at the end. I get it all. She throws her arms in the air and her mom materializes beside her, picking her up. She gives the girl a kiss on the cheek and then helps her back up the stairs in case she wants to go again. And she does. Five more times. I'll give them the photos later—her mom loves when I capture her daughter having fun.

After a few minutes, I realize I've stopped taking pictures and am just watching. That was me at one time, scared and giddy, confused and determined. The slide was the biggest problem to me. And my mom was always there to kiss my cheek and tell me I did a great job, even when I didn't quite make it down.

I think back to my search and wonder—would it have been the same with my birth mother? Would she have taken me to the park and helped me face my fears? Would I have turned out the same, had my life been with her? Would I be me?

I twist my camera's lens, thinking. I know I don't want a different life, but that doesn't keep me from wondering.

I push off the post and head to Java Jump. Celine will be waiting, and though I know she won't have answers, she might, at least, have distractions.

TWO

I open the door and see Celine right away. Her back straight and tall, she's chatting with the barista at the counter. She has her large, black-rimmed glasses on, and once again I am envious of the way style and cuteness come so easy to her.

"Hey," I say when I get to the counter. The barista—a guy a bit older than us with sandy-brown hair and similar glasses—does the hello nod, and looks back at Celine. She smiles at me and says, "Oh, hey" very casually. I suddenly wonder if she invited me here just to be nice, and didn't actually intend for me to come. A blush crosses my face, and I make a gesture toward the end of the line.

I am an idiot sometimes.

After a few seconds, she comes over to me. "Hey, sorry!"

"No, sorry for interrupting," I say, waving my hand.

"Oh, don't worry about it. He's a friend of my older brother. Cute, isn't he? He just started working here, so, you know, excuse to get more coffee or whatever," she says with a smile. And it's in that moment that I miss Treena. Like me, she hasn't had a boyfriend. We used to talk about the whole world of flirting, and how we weren't very good at it.

"Very cute," I say instead, and she grins.

We get iced coffee and sit in the corner, where she has a good view of the counter. I feel my phone vibrate and see it's my mom asking where I am. I text her back a quick explanation, and then tune in to Celine.

"So I've been thinking about my project."

"Yeah?" I say, taking a sip of my drink.

"I think I'm going to do that thing where I re-create photos of my brothers and sisters and me. You know, like, find old ones and have us pose the same way again. Kind of showing how we've grown and stuff. So the whole family-changes-but-not-really angle. What do you think?"

I think of the photo I was looking at earlier of the ice-skating rink and answer, "I think it's a really cute idea. I've seen it done before, but not in class. I think it'll be fun."

"What about you?" she asks, looking me over casually, then back down at her drink. "Any thoughts after class?"

"Tons, really, but none that amount to anything. Family to me means my parents. But there's an entire other side that feels like it would make the project incomplete if I didn't include it."

Celine nods, and suddenly, a song comes on that Treena and I used to sing along to all the time on the way to school—like, annoyingly loud. Naturally, I smile and start moving my head to the beat of the song. My mind goes to her, now at Florida State University, being the college girl. And then I realize the connection. "Oh my gosh."

"What?" Celine asks.

"Sorry, hold on a second," I say, not wanting to stop my thoughts from coming. I let the idea rush over me, and tell her, "I just had the best idea. I can't believe I hadn't thought of it before."

"What?" she asks.

"I was adopted in Tallahassee. Treena's in college in Tallahassee."

"So you're gonna go visit her?" she asks, swirling her straw around her drink.

"Yeah," I muse. "I mean, I'll try to. Maybe I can go up there and find something on my birth mother."

"That's pretty cool," she says. "Have you tried Googling her?"

"Yeah, of course, but nothing. But maybe if I'm up there . . ."

"You can find something in person," she says, eyeing me, then looking briefly over at the guy back at the counter. Celine's a good friend, but my best friend is a phone call away.

I hold my thoughts for a little longer and Celine tells

me about her plans for the weekend, and this movie she saw about vampires that was very explicit. I listen, but really my mind is going as fast as it can.

After a while, I finally make my excuse to leave. "Hey, my mom's waiting for me. Talk later?"

"Yeah, of course," Celine says. "Let me know what you decide for your project. I'm gonna go talk up the barista," she says, wiggling her eyebrows. "Baristo? I don't know."

"'Guy at the counter' works well, too." I smile.

My phone is in my hands the minute I'm outside.

It rings for an excruciating second before Treena picks up.

"MAUDE!" she literally yells into the phone, and I count down until she launches into her typical second sentence. "AHH! When are you visiting?"

"That's actually why I'm calling," I say. Just hearing her voice makes me feel better, more me and less a floating buoy with no one to cling on to.

"WHAT! Oh my gosh, details," she continues, and I laugh at her excitement. It's always there. She's always turned up a few degrees more than everyone else, and it makes everything with her an adventure; I mean, even going to the library.

"Okay, well, it's not set in stone or anything, and I haven't even asked my parents yet, but I have an idea that I want to run by you first."

"Yes, please," she says, and I can hear wind in the background. She's outside like me, probably walking to or from class as I walk home. We're in different areas, but our lives are still parallel.

"So I have to do this photography project on family," I begin, then tell her about my idea of looking for my birth mother.

"Wow. That's really cool," she says when I'm done, more gently than normal, and I know she's worried. I know she's thinking about what this all means.

"This won't be like last time," I tell her, referring to the time that I just started calling people with the last name of Fullman who lived in Tallahassee. I was fourteen and angry and she helped me put the phone down. She was always good at that—being there for me through the hard stuff, but stopping me when it was time.

"No, I know, that was a million years ago." She pauses. "I'm all in, and I'm totally going to help you, you know that...."

"But..."

She hesitates again, then sighs. "Okay, I love you, and that's the only reason why I'm saying this."

"I know what you're going to say. You're worried."

"You've been down this road before. I'm just afraid you won't find anything again."

I sigh, disheartened, as she states my fear out loud. "I know." I nod, even though she can't see. "It's totally a possibility. But I think there's something there, I really do. I don't know, I want to try."

"I know, I get it. And I think you should, I'm just—"

"Playing mom?" I joke, referring to how she always took the role of mom when we would play house growing up. How she kind of turned out that way, always watching over her friends, always there to take care of me when needed.

"You love it," she says, and I laugh.

"I do. And I can't wait to see you!"

"I KNOW! Oh my god, it's going to be so much fun. I can't wait to show you around! And show you off! And everything!" Treena says. And I smile. Because, yeah, she knows when to stop me or caution me. But like the time she sat in the car with me the first day I got my license, she's also always there to hold my hand and take my mind off things when I'm ready to go.

And I'm ready.